<u>The Boys From Clarey Ave</u>

By Michelle Ann Cramer Batson

Distributed by Lulu
www.lulu.com

ISBN: 978-0-578-05635-7

First Edition: April 2010

www.MichelleAnnCramer.Com

Contact Author - CramerBooks@aol.com

For
Mike, Steve, Jeff, Brett
and of course, Kelley

Special thanks to Brett, Jana, Mom and Mattie for their
help in writing this book; Great ideas, great characters
and great, helpful editing.

Special dedication to the kids of Westmoreland School.
Especially the Class of '92.'
Thanks for being such characters!

Attention Readers! This story is FICTION!
Although the characters are mostly modeled after
real people, and a few of the events did actually
take place…they did not all happen to these people
in real life. This is a story. It was completely made
up in my mind…please respect it as nothing more
than that… a fictional story about a small boy and
the people he meets along his fictional way.

If you are truly interested in finding out what is real
and what is not, please check my Website for
clarity!

www.MichelleAnnCramer.Com

Table of Contents

Chapter   **Page #**

1. The New Kid   11

2. Don't Sing in The Bathroom   25

3. Clarey Ave   33

4. Through The Glass   39

5. Goin' Fishin'   53

6. House Hunting   67

7. So, Do you like her?   75

8. The History Lesson in The Mess Hall   85

9. Be A Man   97

10. Shut Up Phil   103

11. Fire and ~~Ice~~ *Mailboxes*?   115

12. Damsel In Distress   125

13. 3 A.M   133

14. Get A Grip   141

15. Every Action   145

16. Do You Smell That?   153

17. Movin' On   161

This is a story about nothing.

Lucas Reed often thinks about the year that he and his family lived in Upstate New York as the year that changed his life. His time spent in Hampton Mills, and at J.D.W. School was a time when he realized the person that he was, and how to become the person that he really wanted to be.

It was a year filled with great adventure, and even greater friendships.

It's funny though, when he thinks back on those days, he realizes that nothing great actually happened. There was no championship football game to win, no group protest to save some tree, no mystery that needed to be solved in the knick of time. In fact nothing of any importance happened at all.

When he retells the stories of his year in Hampton Mills, he very quickly realizes that the stories aren't even really about him. They're tales of brotherhood, and of belonging. It's the only place he ever completely felt like he fit in. And most of his stories, Lucas finds, are about *them*, and what he learned from being surrounded by them...

The boys from Clarey Ave.

The New Kid 1

Fall 1984

Lucas Reed stood in the long desolate hallway with his hands clasped in front of him and body turned towards the wall. He drew in a deep cringing breath as he heard the faint sound of footsteps quickly approaching him from behind. Afraid to exhale, he tried not to cry as his lower lip chewing began; the last thing that he needed was to be found the way he was, *and* crying. *Crybaby,* he thought, would be a kind nickname compared to the others that could come from this situation. He saw the red haired boy out of the corner of his eye as he strolled by him with indifference. Lucas started to slowly let out his breath in relief when the boy stopped, turned in Lucas' direction and looked at him quizzically. Walking just a few steps towards him, the boy coolly lifted his chin in the air to him, in what everyone on the planet recognizes as the universal sign for, 'what's up.'

Lucas could feel the tears welling up again as his body started to sweat. He averted his eyes looking to the ground as his breaths became short and quick. The red haired boy began walking towards the new kid that clung to the hallway wall.

"Hey. You okay?"

Lucas nodded silently, afraid to look up, while he twisted his hands in discomfort.

"Kid. You need help or something?"

Lucas placed his forehead against the cool ceramic tiles and turned his body inward even more. A large black poster taped to the wall next to him that read, *Just say NO,* as his heart pounded loudly in his chest. How would he get out of this unscathed; without anyone finding out what he had done?

The red haired boy turned his body back down the hall in the direction he was originally headed, "you want me to get a teacher or something?" he asked skeptically.

"No." Lucas cried out with certainty.

"Then what's up man? What are you doing?"

Lucas took a deep breath as he closed his eyes. He had always been a firm believer, that if you couldn't see them, then maybe they couldn't see you. No matter how many times in life he tried it though, it never seemed to work. He opened his eyes and the boy was still there.

The red haired boy became agitated. He clearly had somewhere to be and was risking trouble himself, so he gave it one last try, "listen, I gotta get to the office. I'm already in trouble. Do you need help or not?"

Lucas shook his head reaching up to wipe his eye which had finally surrendered just one single drop. Moving his clenched hands, he revealed his secret. The tall, skinny fifth grader with his bright red hair noticed what this strange boy was hiding. He hesitated only for a second. If he was affected by it at all, he never let on. Instead, he looked around for help, noticing a door a few feet ahead, he tried the knob; it was unlocked.

"Get in here," he said motioning to the scared little boy.

Lucas himself quickly looked around and saw no one else in sight. He quickly ducked into the room closing the door behind him that read, 'supply closet' on the outside.

The red haired boy ran through the very long hallway all the way back to his classroom. He stopped just short of his room and ducked down past the windowed door, careful not to be seen. He reached into his blue metal locker and closed it carefully and quietly behind him. He ducked once again past the classroom door, and again he was off; running quickly but carefully so not to get caught until he reached the supply closet. He knocked once before opening the door. He passed the item to Lucas and closed the door behind him, darting off to the principle's office.

The next day Lucas stepped down from the yellow school bus and fought his way through the crowded mess of kindergartners, that were supposed to represent a line. He ventured down that same long hallway, past the library, the art room and of course the supply closet. It seemed to take forever as the herd of children moved through the building like sheep filing to their pens. Finally he reached the fifth grade rooms. Quickly he pulled his backpack off his shoulder and scanned the crowd. It took him only seconds to spot him towering over the group of boys. The same red headed boy that had come to his aid the day before was only a few feet away. He reached into his pack to return the boy's possession. Lucas shoved his backpack into the locker, wadding the item up in his hands as small as he could and waited for the bell. When the ring summoning them to class finally sounded he moved quickly, almost stealth-like amongst the kids towards the boy, reaching for his arm. The boy stopped and looked strangely at him. He had never really gotten a good look at Lucas' face in the hallway the previous day. Lucas handed up the wad reminding him who he was. The boy smirked and nodded taking his gym shorts from him.

No one had said anything to Lucas that morning, of course that was not unusual. It was to his relief that there were no whispers and no finger pointing. Lucas felt fairly certain that the kid had not told any one of his plight the day before. He sat down at his desk and waited for the second bell to start their day.

At lunch time he took his brown paper sack and went straight to a table he noticed was empty. It was day four in the new school, and still no one had spoken to him. He looked into the sack to see what his mother had sent with him, but only took out one item at a time in case anyone told him to move, or worse came over to bully him for his lunch. He had learned the hard way in first grade not to display your lunch when you are the new kid. He pulled out his jelly sandwich from its plastic entrapment and took a bite. Still very nervous he sat timidly, struck with the notion that all eyes were on the 'new kid.' Three bites into his sandwich, he felt a presence walk up behind him. *Oh Crap,* he thought. Lucas stopped chewing as he braced for what could very well be a shove from behind. Instead, the person set their metal lunch box down on the white table top and straddled the bench next to him. "Hey."

Lucas looked at the blue lunch box with Batman on the front, then moved his eyes to the person sitting to his right. Once again, it was the red haired boy. Lucas gave a closed lipped smiled since the jelly soaked bread was stuck firmly to the roof of his mouth.

"Brett," the kid said as he stuck out his right hand.

Lucas grabbed on and pumped it twice as he tried to swallow, "ucas," he said with a full mouth.

"What?" the boy laughed.

"Oh sorry. Lucas. Lucas Reed."

"Good to meet ya."

He was Brett Wilson - the tallest kid in the whole fifth grade. He was skinny as a rail, with Irish pale skin chocked full of freckles. His hair was wildly curly and always scattered carelessly about. The red mess seemed to somehow grow upwards rather then down like most peoples hair, making him seem even taller then he actually was.

Brett looked at the sack lunch, "what'cha eatin'?"

Lucas shrugged it off, "nothing." He hated peanut butter with his jelly, but thought that made him weird, so he never told anyone it was just jelly.

"After lunch we play dodge ball, you wanna come?" he asked.

"Yeah. Thanks," he responded as coolly as he could. Lucas was thrilled and ready to toss his whole lunch to run outside right away, but he had been working hard to master the cool, uninterested approach for *this* new school. Every time the Reed family moved and he changed schools, he fully took advantage of the opportunity to reinvent himself. This *Cool Lucas* was maybe starting to work. Not only had someone spoken to him, but he actually asked him to hangout with him *and* his friends.

The friendly kid tore into his lunchbox, the lid clinking against the table. He had a bologna sandwich, potato chips and a giant chocolate chip cookie. He started with the cookie. "So where'd you move here from?"

"River."

"You like it better there?"

Lucas shrugged, "I dunno. I mean its school right?"

"You're small. I didn't think you were in fifth grade," he said.

Lucas nodded as he bit his front teeth through the rind of his orange.

"Maybe you *shouldn't* play dodge ball," Brett laughed.

Lucas looked up from his orange, "I'll be alright. Don't worry about me."

Brett nodded as he reached into the bag of chips, "cool."

The small dark haired boy had peeled his orange and was putting each slice on his tongue one at a time. Silently counting down to zero in his head, he chomped down on each one, exploding them like grenades in his mouth. Finally he had to ask, "so, what were you in trouble for?"

"What?" Brett asked.

"Yesterday. You were going to the office?"

"Oh," Brett smiled and nodded. He looked around to make sure no cafeteria aids were watching. "Neil and I were doing this," he said folding his arms up, touching his fists to his shoulders. "We were doing that and telling everyone we had boobs like Dolly Parton," he laughed again.

Lucas laughed for the first time at J.D.W. Elementary. "Of course, Neil didn't get caught. Just me," Brett added.

"Wha'd they do to ya?"

Brett laughed through his nose as if mocking the pathetic attempt to punish such a nothing crime, "two days after school detention."

Both boys finished their lunches and quickly chugged down their twenty five cent carton of milk. They collected their trash with the playground in their sights. Lucas threw out his sack and waited for Brett to put his lunch box away. Then together they exited the cafeteria. They found the group of kids just starting to gather on the black top behind the gym, tossing around the large red balls.

"Hey guys," Brett said to the motley fifth grade crew. "This is Luke."

They all nodded to him and gave a few 'heys,' as if they really cared. They stood in a group as Brett and Brian walked out from the crowd and started calling out names. *Great,* Lucas thought, *picking teams. Wonder who will be picked last.*

Brian went first picking Steve, followed by Brett choosing Neil. Brian went again and selected Sonny. Brett took his time as he studied the gaggle. Raising his hand to his chin and resting it carefully on top, he appeared to be carefully pondering his next choice, "Luke," he finally said with a smile.

Lucas stood there starring off into space. He stood tall to appear confident, but secretly he was dieing inside. He could literally feel himself sweating from head to toe as he knew he would be left as the last one standing there; no one would want the new kid.

"Luke," Brett called out again. Lucas was struck out of his trance. *Oh my god. They didn't pick me last*, he realized in shock.

He trotted over next to Neil and waited victoriously. Finally the last kid was picked. Lucas felt bad for BJ, but somebody had to be chosen last and at least it wasn't him. Both Brett and Brian stood facing each other as each curled up their right fist. They shook it twice and on three, threw out their selection. It was Rock, Paper, Scissors and the best two out of three won. The loser's team would be first against the wall.

Brett lost. *Great,* Lucas though. They walked over and lined up against the brick backside of the gymnasium.

"Don't get hit in the temple," he heard from his right side. Jason Sharper had leaned over to give him advice. "If you get hit in the temple," he paused to brace himself for the attack, "you'll die."

Lucas looked at him in shock. Jason nodded as he chewed on his lower lip. "It's true man. I ain't lyin'."

Lucas' eyes had grown as big as quarters as he turned himself back towards the firing squad that had already armed themselves. The word was given and the balls started flying. Lucas was remarkably wirey. He dodged the first three balls that were all aimed at him, and then he caught the next one, taking Eric out of the game! Just as that great move was accomplished, he was nailed in the side; by BJ, who glared at him with contempt.

Lucas took his seat on the sidelines and watched as his team was wiped out one by one, until only Brett, their captain, remained. Finally, after each one had re-armed, they belted him all at once, yelling as they released their cash of ammunition. He was out.

Brett's team got to their feet, wiping the loose stone from their backsides and collecting the bouncing red balls. Brian's team took their place against the wall. 'Ready, set, go,' started the launch. Everyone throwing the balls violently at the kids lined up against the brick wall. Lucas first aimed randomly, but his second ball had BJ's name on it. He hit him square in the gut. He bent over, reaching for his stomach as he walked to the sideline. Lucas felt good about himself, he didn't care if he even picked up another ball...they were even.

The game ended as recess drew to a close. The group of kids gathered around together laughing at who got hit and where. Finally Lucas spoke up, "you guys don't play dodge ball like I ever have."

Brian looked at the new kid sizing him up, "how do you play?"

Lucas shrugged, once again as he reminded himself to play it cool. "We usually line the balls up in the middle of the two teams. Then we dive for them and start whaling on each other." Lucas smiled with a little laugh, "this way's fun though."

"Where you from?" Jason Sharper asked.

"River," he answered.

"Where you live now?"

"On some little circle: Landit Manor."

"That's cool. Brett and I live right around the corner from ya," Jason informed him. He looked over at the gangly red head, "a lotta' ways to get in trouble in Hampton Mills," he said with a mischievous grin.

Brett gave the same devilish smile and walked away.

The bell rang and they headed once again in a herd, back into the school. It was time for history, Lucas' favorite subject. Being a Military Brat, he had lived his lifetime surrounded by everything that was American history and loved very much to learn about the different wars.

When school finally ended, he once again found himself on the bus. He looked around for Brett wondering if all this time he had been only a few seats away. His unmistakable red head was no where in sight. Jason Sharper however was sitting in the back of the bus with his buddies. Afraid to push his luck, he took a seat in the middle with some kid that smelled very much like a foot. Lucas sat contently with his bag in his lap. He felt pretty good about his day: he had finally started to make some friends.

The bus came to a stop on the corner of English Road and Landit Manor, where he disembarked and walked quickly home. At moments he felt himself almost in a jog. Darting threw the house he put his bag on his bed and stripped out of his school clothes. Quickly he changed into some older play clothes and beat up Pony sneakers. Careful to avoid any long conversations about whether or not he had made friends, he snuck out the side door into the garage. He mounted his blue BMX bicycle and headed out to explore the neighborhood.

Right around the corner, he thought to himself. Both Brett and Jason lived here in Hampton Mills - now just to find them. He had decided earlier during study period, that he would ride around appearing bored and uninterested hoping to casually bump into them.

He peddled quickly to the stop sign on English Road, where he halted his bike before continuing on. As he waited for a car to pass, he noticed a dog directly across the street from him. A large tan colored dog sat in the corner lot on guard. *Good doggie,* he thought as he stared at the dirty mutt. Lucas then spotted something moving across the street on his left. Sitting on the other corner, was yet another dog; a smaller brown dog, with thick, furry, Chow like hair. They looked across the street at one another, and Lucas was certain he saw one wink at the other before they both looked back at him. *Oh crap,* he thought as his heart began to race. Both dogs stood up from their squatting positions and started moving towards him. Lucas quickly rounded the corner of English Road and North Street and peddled hard, never looking back. As he sped down North Street, an old blue car rumbled by. With a sizable hole in the muffler making it deafening, he thought that he heard someone yell something to him as it went by. As the car pulled further away, he saw four boys packed inside. *Jerks,* he thought.

He rode up and down North Street, staying clear of the killer dogs. He ventured down a few side roads, reading the names on the few mailboxes that there were. He saw no one that looked familiar and nothing that jumped out at him as to where these boys might live.

Hampton Mills was divided by the bridge - J.D.W. School District on one side, and Rowing Park School District was on the other. His mother had given him boundaries the very first day that they moved into town, and the bridge was as far as he was allowed to travel. Lucas spent a good hour trolling the neighborhood to no avail. With great disappointment, Lucas finally decided that it was a wasted effort. If they had wanted to hang out with him, they would have asked.

Lucas stopped one last time at the bridge and turned himself back around. As he found his way back towards English Road, that same blue car came barreling out of a dead end street. Just past the church was a small street with three houses on it and a baseball field at the end of the road. The car turned left and headed away from Lucas yet again. This time he noticed only one person in the car; a larger male with one hand on the steering wheel while the other feathered his hair.

Don't Sing in The Bathroom 2

The next morning Lucas boarded the bus that came through the Manor. He took a random seat in the middle section and waited to see who might sit next to him. So far he was alone. He watched Christina Stampard, another fifth grader proudly show off her new Cabbage Patch doll, with blue eyes and dimpled cheeks. She glowed as if she had given birth to it herself, as her friends admired her blonde braided hair and paisley dress. Lucas rolled his eyes and silently mocked, *girls*.

The bus drove up North Street and stopped in front of the church parking lot where a large group of kids stood awaiting their ride. The bus doors opened and Lucas counted eleven kids trudging up the stairs. He quickly spotted Jason Sharper's shaggy blond head. Jason had a certain way about him. At first, he appeared to be a tad on the dorky side, but as you watched him with his friends you very quickly came to realize that his awkwardness was the very thing that somehow made him cool. He was unique, and instead of being made fun of, his quirks were actually embraced. Jason was any average skinny kid with beach boy blond hair, almost white, that always hung shagged in his blue eyes. His skin was still tanned from the summer sun, but what stood out the most for Jason was his walk. It had kind of a heavy footed side to side motion that you would expect from a fat kid. But he wasn't fat. He just had a kind of waddle to him.

Jason walked right down the aisle as if he had made the trip a million times before. He noticed Lucas and smiled hello, as he sat himself down in the seat beside him. "Hey. What's up?" he asked.

"Hey." Lucas said as cool and collected as he could. His heart was light, and he felt as though his whole body was grinning. *Be cool*, he kept telling himself.

Brett was a few kids behind Jason and planted himself into the seat across the aisle. He leaned over to say something to Jason when he noticed the new kid, "Luke man. What's up?" he asked with that same universal chin gesture.

"Hey." Lucas replied with the same distant cool tone as before.

Continuing a conversation that started before they mounted the bus, Brett quietly said to Jason, "so. What are we gonna do about him?"

Jason starred over the seat tops into space with his mouth loosely open, and then completely out of the blue he had a response, "let's hold him down and fart on his head," he said with a laugh.

Brett laughed heartily as he held his stomach and threw himself against the green seat back. Then reaching his left hand up under his t-shirt, he cupped his hand against his armpit and proceeded with the farting noises.

On cue, Jason placed his palm against his mouth and too created the do it yourself fart. The whole bus was roaring with laughter as they all attempted their best gas impressions. Even a few girls joined in, that is except for Christina and her friends who were, trying to protect *the baby.*

The yellow beast was soon spinning out of control, forcing the school bus driver to pull off to the side of the road. Putting the bus into park Mrs. Flynn stood up and faced her rowdy passengers. Her look alone was all that was needed. The children took one glance at her cold, expressionless face and they were silent. Finding themselves back in their seats they quietly prepared for the remainder of the ride.

It didn't take long before Jason was bored, "So Luke. Lucas…Luuucasss….." he leaned his head towards the new kid, motioning with his hand as if he wanted something from him.

Lucas leaned towards him with raised brow. *Does he want money?* He wondered.

"Your name. Lucas what?"

Lucas sat back with enlightenment, "Oh. Reed. Lucas Reed."

"Reeeed…" he said nodding his head rhythmically.

Wait for it, he thought to himself. Lucas was certain what would fall next from Jason's mouth.

"Can you read, *Reed?*"

And there it was. Lucas pretended to smile as if it were funny, or even original, but he had heard that a million times.

The bus soon arrived at school. The children all stood up in one single motion as the bus jilted to a stop. Filing down the steps and once again through the kindergarteners, they headed to the furthest wing of the school. Stuffing their bags into their lockers the bell rang and class began.

Mr. Rockwell was a tall, slim man, with thinning hair on top and large glasses. He announced after the Pledge of Allegiance that morning, that they would be visiting the nurse for their checkups. This meant hearing, eyesight, scoliosis and of course, lice; first the girls and then the boys.

They pulled out their math books and began their lesson on fractions. Lucas looked around the room as his mind wandered from the black board to the alphabet scrolling above it. He thought to himself, *seriously, this is fifth grade. If you don't know those by now, you're an idiot.* As he read through the letters down to 'Z' he noticed the purple poster at the end with Garfield on it.

FOR EVERY ACTION THERE IS AN EQUAL
AND OPPOSITE REACTION.

Lucas furrowed his brow as he thought about what that meant, then shrugged it off. His attention was quickly brought to the classroom door as it opened and three girls passed through silently. The door closed and next he read the poster under the window.

IGNORANCE IS NOT BLISS

What the heck does that mean?

"OK gentleman," Mr. Rockwell addressed the class, breaking into Lucas' poster contemplations.

The school nurse was standing at the door waiting to escort them to her office. She was a short older woman with a white lab coat, thick glasses and short graying hair sticking out from under her nurse's cap. She smiled revealing the lipstick on her teeth, as the boys stood and formed a line in front of her.

Once at her office they entered another small room one at a time to be checked. They started with the eye chart, and then they lifted their shirts as she checked their spine for any curvature. Sitting back down she checked through their hair for lice and finally they were fitted with headphones for the hearing test. As they finished raising their hands at the sound of the tones in their ears, they were sent back to their classroom.

Alphabetically Lucas was always towards the end of the list. He was checked out and excused back to class. The nurse's aid stopped him as he headed for the door and handed him a piece of paper, asking him to deliver it to a second grade teacher. Unfamiliar with that wing of the school, he took the sheet and curiously set out alone on his adventure. He turned at the cafeteria, and walked past the office which was directly across from the front doors. He continued down that short hallway reading the names on each door. As he passed by the door on his left, he heard a faint noise that sounded very much like singing from inside of a little room. Finally, he found Mrs. Mattison's

room. He knocked gently on the door. The sweet
young teacher came to the door in her pretty dress
and pearls tied around her neck. She graciously
took the slip of paper with a smile and thanked him.
Lucas smiled at her pleasant demeanor then turned
himself around to return to class. He got only a few
feet when he heard the commotion across the hall.

The teacher was a short older woman. Not older
like most teachers, but older like *too old*. She
appeared to be a grumpy old woman with coke
bottle glasses and a mean sneer on her wrinkled
face. She was a rude awakening from the pleasant
second grade teacher he had just met. In her hand, a
wooden paddle! It all happened so quickly that
Lucas could barely react. He saw her whip open the
bathroom door in her classroom. From inside the
bathroom he heard a gasp and a little girl cry out!
Just as quickly as she opened the door, the girl was
yanked from inside with her pants still down around
her knees. She yelled at her to pull up her pants as
she dragged her out in front of the entire class!

"This is what happens to you when you sing in the
bathroom," he heard the nasty old woman say; as
she lay the little blonde girl across her lap and she
smacked her with the wooden paddle! The girl
screamed.

Lucas gasped in shock! Never had he seen such a
thing. He turned his head back down the hallway
and beat feet for his own classroom. He did not
want to witness anymore, and more importantly he
did not want to get taken over her knee in front of
the first graders. Lucas walked as fast as he could;
past the office, down the long corridor (which he

could not travel down without glaring at the supply
closet) and back into his classroom. Silently he
took his seat. He picked up his pencil and worked
as hard as he could to actually learn something.

On this day for lunch he decided on a different approach. Rather than trying to be first and seeing who would sit with him, he hung back. He wanted to see the other kids sit down and see if anyone invited him to join. He stood in line for his milk and tried to see around the kids in front of him. He weaved back and forth and tipped up on his toes repeatedly to see where kids were sitting. *This could go very wrong*, he thought. He stepped out of the kitchen doorway and glanced quickly around the room. *Just go sit with them ya wuss,* he told himself. He walked in the direction of the fifth grade boys he had played dodge ball with the day before. The walk seemed to take forever. He felt with every step the table actually seemed to be farther away. As he held his brown bag and milk in one hand and he struggled to put his money in his pocket with the other, he was suddenly struck from behind. A kid blew past him running aggressively into his arm.

"Come on Reader," he heard as he was swearing silently in his mind at the clumsy jerk. It was Jason again. He was inviting him to sit with them. Lucas took a deep breath of relief and tried to hide his excitement as he quickly averted his eyes to the ground so no one would see them smile. Then he stood up straight and confidently walked over to their table. He stepped over the bench and sat down with the gang. *He was in.*

Recess and the rest of the day went by uneventfully. On the bus ride home Brett, once again was not on board. Lucas sat this time across the aisle from

Jason and laughed hysterically as he watched him continually reach over the seat and stick his spit ridden finger into the ear of the smaller kid in front of him. The little kid was tough and never cried, but the fun stopped when his sixth grade sister came back to sit with him.

After the bus ride, Lucas did as he had the day before. He went home quickly, changed his clothes and snuck out through the garage to avoid his mother's inquisition. Back on his bike, he rode through Hampton Mills. Today he knew at least where to look. Both Brett and Jason boarded the bus together from the church parking lot, so they had to live close to that stop. Ten years old and on a mission; down English Road, right onto North Street, and straight towards the church. He passed the row of houses and the small garage where the older local men seemed to gather all day long.

The dark haired boy finally reached the church parking lot and slowed his bike as he pulled in off the main road. He looked quickly around, but again saw no sign of any other children. *The baseball field*, he thought to himself. Back into action, he peddled down the dead end street towards the baseball field behind the Parish Hall. As he reached the end of the road, he skid his bike to a stop kicking up loose stones. Nobody. 'Crap,' he said to himself quietly. Lucas took a deep breath and exhaled a depressing sigh as he turned his bike back around.

With the wind gone from his sails, he rolled slowly down the small avenue, when a car turned the corner between the Church and the Parish Hall's parking lot. It began crawling down the street towards him…loudly. It was the same blue car that roared past him the day before. It looked menacing to Lucas as the blue beast loudly slithered towards the small boy, with its four troublesome looking passengers inside. Lucas rode to the left side of the road, close to the brick building and stopped. He felt confident that if he needed to get away he could either jump the sidewalks or in a worst case scenario, he could toss the bike and run through the field back to the Manor. The blue bomber stopped short and stared down upon him…it seemed to linger at him as it sat rumbling in the road. His chest got tight…*fight or flight,* he thought to himself. *Do I run now or wait and see what happens?* Then, uneventfully, the car turned left and pulled into the first driveway of the large two story home right behind the church. Lucas' brow furrowed once again, "What are they doing?" He quietly said. Then it occurred to him, *oh my God. That's where they live. I am literally on their turf…they're gonna kill me!*

Certain that his young life was about to end tragically, Lucas sat motionless. He had a clear escape route through the field, or he could 'man up' and drive right on by, essentially driving straight into the battle. But he waited. He was not brought up to ever be a 'scaredy cats.' He had never been taught to ever run in the face of a conflict. It was a better plan to observe his surroundings for every possible advantage for once the battle began, and to size up his opponent for strengths and weaknesses.

He watched as the boys filed out of the blue car. The driver was a big guy. He looked to be about sixteen or seventeen years old with feathered strawberry colored hair. He was tall and lean, wearing his varsity football jersey. The shotgun rider opened the passenger side door and stepped out as well. This one was not as tall, and unlike the other, he had curly blonde hair, but was just as lean. He laughed at something as he exited the vehicle in his stone washed jeans with a higher pitched girl like giggle. Another boy climbed out from behind the driver's seat. He looked close in size and age to the blonde kid. He was very average, like any fourteen year old-ish kid would look with short auburn hair and a skinny face. The three boys walked around the front of the car as the last kid climbed out from the backseat. Slipping under the passenger side seat belt stepped a younger skinny kid with red hair. Lucas was taken back as he recognized this last kid. It was Brett Wilson. *Was this where he lived,* he wondered. Then in a sigh of relief he thought, *maybe I'm not gonna die today.*

The boys never noticed Lucas. He watched as Brett grabbed his books from the car and they all walked inside their house oblivious to the fight they were almost in. Lucas saw them all the way inside before he began to peddle back down the road. He rolled slowly by and glanced in the garage, then sized up the house and yard. He noticed the many bikes laying about, the doll on the side steps, the tire swing hanging from the tree in the side yard, and the dog house presently without a dog. Lucas rode to the stop sign at the end of the road where it bumped into North Street. He sat there for a moment wondering why he didn't stop or yell out to the red haired boy. Then he looked up at the road sign clearly marking the intersection of North Street and Clarey Ave. He glanced right, then left, and then turned towards home.

The next day after school, Lucas thought he might try again. He rushed home to change, climbed on the blue BMX bike and peddled through town. On this day he encountered that same mangy brown dog, however this time, the dog was strutting down the opposite side of the road. Lucas didn't feel that he was engaging him, so he kept his eyes forward and pressed onward.

Because he did not see the blue car in the driveway, he first rode past Clarey Ave,. He continued on to the bridge, stopping just short of it and turning back around. As he U-turned his bike he encountered a small pile of gravel on the shoulder of the road, that someone had obviously attempted to make into a jump. He leaned down into his handle bars and peddled hard. Aiming for the center, he drove up and over the stone pile and flew through the air... *Might as well, Jump!* He was certain he heard Van Halen singing their anthem as he hung suspended in the air. Landing, he turned his bike around and went back to do it again. He was soaring. Lucas Reed was flying high above North Street...well, he went at least a foot and a half.

Lucas had forgotten why he was visiting this side of town at all, when he suddenly spotted the car coming towards him. Once again he was looking into the grill of the rumbling blue beast. Lucas choked up on the bars and pushed hard for Clarey Ave. *I have to get there in time for Brett to see me,* he thought to himself as he rode his heart out. He reached the Church parking lot as the car was turning towards home. His first instinct was to cut through the parking lot, but that would put him right in their yard, and make him seem too needy. He wanted to be aloof…to seem casual, and for their meeting to appear accidental.

He turned down Clarey Ave very carefully, slowing his pace as he heard the engine cut and saw the driver's door open. *I'm gonna miss him,* he worried as he sped back up. He rolled down the blacktop avenue, and right on past as he saw Brett exiting the car. The red haired boy never looked up. *Damn it. He missed me.* Lucas casually rode to the baseball field, made another casual U-turn, and tried to once again, *casually,* roll past.

"Luke?"

It worked!!! But Lucas did not react immediately. He slowed the bicycle and looked around in every direction but towards Brett, as he heard his name again.

"Luke." this time spoken with confidence.

He put on his breaks and placed his foot to the ground. Turning around he spotted the red haired boy on his porch steps. Tilting his head to the side and squinting (although, he didn't know why) he called back, "Brett?"

Brett came down off the porch and walk towards the street, as Lucas rolled over to meet him half way. They met in the middle of Clarey Ave on the yellow line that divided it.

"Whata you doin'?" Brett asked him.

Cool..., he reminded himself as his excitement was trying to boil over from the inside. Taking a deep breath, he shrugged his shoulders and gave the 'nothin' sideways head toss. Looking around, he added, "Just lookin' for something to do around here."

"You're kidding right? There's a million things to do here."

"Like what?" Lucas asked.

"Oh man, I don't know," he told him. "Come on. I wanna grab a snack, and then we'll find some trouble to get into."

YES!!! Lucas wanted to cry out into the crisp fall air! But he was casual. He nodded and followed Brett back to his house on his bike. He carefully placed it between the house and the garage on its kickstand, and then followed him inside of the large two story home.

Standing in the Kitchen was the darker haired boy he had seen the day before. As he tied his sneaker onto his foot, Brett pointed to him and informed, "That's my brother, Dave." Dave looked up and said 'hey,' as he grabbed his coat and walked out the door. Lucas smiled up at him as he blew past, and then watched through the glass as Dave got into a car that had pulled into the lot across the street.

Brett opened the stove door and pulled out a box of pizza. Tossing it nonchalantly on the kitchen table he pushed up the box top. There was one slice left. "You wanna split it?" he asked.

Lucas peered down at the crusty slice of day old pizza, and shook his head no, "that's ok."

"That last slice of pizza's mine!" they heard shouted from up the stairs. Brett looked up from the slice at his new friend. Grinning devilishly, he reached for it as someone moved quickly down the stairs. "Brett! I'm serious. I got dibs!" Lucas recognized the voice from the day before as the blonde kid.

Brett grabbed the pizza and ran through the house. He darted into the living room and stood on the opposite side of the coffee table. The blonde kid reached the bottom step and walked with authority into the living room. There they stood facing off on either side of the table. "Don't even breath on it man," he instructed the freckled face kid. Brett held out the slice in front of his mouth and made taunting eyebrows at him.

"You little Jerk!" he yelled as he moved over the table and grabbed for Brett. Brett dodged his reach and ran quickly back around the table, down the hall and onto the front screen porch. He passed through the porch door as the hungry teenager followed. Once around the blue car in the driveway, Brett dashed back into the house through the side door and locked it behind him.

"Get the porch door!" he yelled to his new friend.

Lucas did as he was instructed and ran onto the screened in porch, locking that door. He returned to the kitchen to find the angry, hungry beast waiting on the other side of the door. Brett waved the cold pizza around in front of him, and then teasingly put it up to his lips. Suddenly, a pale white hand busted through the pane of glass! Cut and beginning to bleed, before anyone could even react, it took the slice from Brett's hand and lips and pulled it back outside. The teenager held it up in front of Brett, and took a bite. "Now open the damn door," he instructed as he chewed victoriously.

Brett unlocked the door and backed away. He returned to the table with Lucas and the empty pizza box, as the blonde haired kid, with crystal blue eyes, walked away with the cold pizza slice.

"That was my brother, Robbie."

Lucas took a deep breath and nodded in recognition. Brett stood up again from the oak table to paw through the cupboards until he finally decided on a snack. He grabbed for the box of chocolate Zingers and offered them to the small boy at the table that had been watching him carefully with his dark eyes. Lucas agreed to the treat so Brett tossed one to him. Next, he watched as the freckled faced kid reached up for two glasses and filled them with Kool-Aid from the fridge. He returned to the table and placed a glass in front of Lucas.

Lucas grabbed it with excitement, "you've got the Ewok glass," he said with probably too much enthusiasm. Brett stopped drinking from his glass and looked quizzically at the boy. "My mom and I were collecting all of these, but we missed the last one…the Ewok glass," he told him pointing to the

Star Wars collectible glass. Brett puckered his lips as he chewed at the inside of his lower cheek and nodded along.

Too much. Lucas quickly recognized he had revealed too much strange information about himself. "Anyway," he shrugged as he tried to make it not such a big deal any longer to him. He picked up his Zinger and struggled with its plastic encasement, as a tiny little person entered through the side door. Stepping carefully through the glass, the young lady in a pink skirt and white ruffled shirt tiptoed her way up to the kitchen table.

"That's Mary Ellen," Brett said as he got up once again from the table and fetched a chocolate Zinger for his little sister. Lucas watched as Brett took the wrapper between his teeth and pulled it open before handing it to her. She smiled at Lucas, and told him it was nice to meet him, before walking away with her snack. *Awe, that was sweet,* he thought to himself, as he watched her tiny little legs carry her away.

Breaking through the 'Norman Rockwell' moment, Lucas heard someone loudly entering like a bull in a China shop from behind him, "What the hell happened here?"

He turned around to meet the largest person he had ever encountered to that point in his life. Towering over top of them and pointing angrily at the door, was the driver of the blue bomber car from the day before. He stood at least six foot four inches tall. He was big and lean as he looked upon Brett for an answer.

"Robbie," was all Brett said, and he took another bite.

"Robbie!" the tall letterman yelled into the other room.

"Brett's cleanin' it up," they heard from the living room.

"What?!" Brett called back to him with surprise.

"You made me do it."

"What?!" he exclaimed again with disgust. "I made you punch through the freakin' window? You're a dumb ass."

"You shouldn't have been fooling around," Robbie told him as he sauntered back into the room rubbing his full stomach.

Brett turned and looked up at his oldest brother pleadingly. The football player took a deep breath and rolled his eyes. "Brett just clean it up. Please."

"What?" Brett revolted.

"Come on. You know he ain't gonna do it. And we're all gonna get in trouble as it is. Just don't let them come home to the mess too."

Brett pushed back from the table angrily as he went to the closet and reached for the broom. He carried it past Robbie with a look to kill. As he placed the broom against the kitchen floor the side door pushed open once again. Brett stepped back annoyingly. "Please. Come right in," he said under his breath.

"What the hell happened here?" Dave Wilson asked as he passed through the doorway.

"I don't freakin' know. But I gotta get to work." The oldest brother, reached over Lucas and grabbed his green work apron off the chair beside him. Lucas crouched down, as the pure stature alone of the big man terrified him.

Brett stopped again as his oldest brother exited the side door, then stopped on the steps and turned back around to Brett. "Thanks," he told him. Brett, who was very angry with him, recognized his sincerity and smiled before he continued sweeping up the mess.

"New kid did it, didn't he?" Dave asked looking at Lucas accusingly. Lucas looked up from his Zinger, which he still had not gotten open, and looked upon him with frightened eyes. Dave winked and smiled at the scared kid.

Chuckling again, Dave said, "I just passed Snoot. He's struttin' through town with Renee Michael's dog." He laughed again at the sight of them, "they look like a couple'a junk yard dogs."

Lucas sat quietly and watched how the dynamics between the brothers played out. Robbie laughed about Snoot, and broke into song. "It's bad, bad, LeRoy Brown, baddest man in the whole damn town." He stopped and pointed to Lucas, "don't ever touch my pizza." He laughed and continued the song, "bigger then old King Kong. Meaner than a junk yard dog," and he danced his way out of the room.

Brett emptied the dust pan outside into the garbage barrel, and came back into the house. Sitting back down across from Lucas, still disgusted, he apologized for the ruckus, "Sorry about that."

Lucas shrugged his shoulders, "that's okay. Who was the big kid?"

"What big kid? Oh. My oldest brother. That's Tommy." Brett stood up one last time and motioned to the new kid, "come on. Let's find something to do"

Together Brett and Lucas ventured outside. They walked behind the Parish Hall, through that small field and found themselves in Jason Sharper's backyard. Jason was quick to greet them and the threesome headed for the woods behind the baseball field.

"We started a new fort out here this past summer," Jason told the new kid.

"We had to after what happened to the last one," Brett added with a smirk.

Jason snickered like a girl.

Lucas laughed at the two of them before asking what had happened.

Jason stopped and faced the kid, with one hand in his jeans pocket and began gesturing wildly with the other, "I'm not gonna give you all the details. But let's just say that Aerosol paint cans and open flames...well they just don't mix well," and he laughed again.

Brett and Lucas both laughed along with the awkward blonde boy as he reenacted the small blaze.

They walked around past the baseball diamond and reached the woods. There they started inward on the beaten path, but then Brett pulled them to a halt. Looking at Jason he asked, "Ya think we can trust him?"

Jason walked around the small boy with his hands once again in each front pocket and looked Lucas up and down. Then he tilted his head and rubbed his still hairless chin.

He nodded.

Brett turned to the side of the path and moved a small piece of brush that had been carefully lain over an opening in the woods. "After you," he said to Lucas gesturing him through the hole.

Lucas passed through and waited. Jason came behind him, followed by Brett who once again, laid the brush hiding the opening. Then moving to the front of the group, Brett led them over three stone steps and a fallen tree. Once on the other side...an entire new beaten path emerged. Lucas' mind drifted to a book he had once read, *The Secret*

Garden. He imagined there would be all sorts of magical things beyond this hole in the shrubs.

As the path led a bit deeper into the woods, it very quickly came to an end. They were there. They reached a wreck of wood and cardboard tossed about into a form of shelter, and they called it their fort. It looked more like a homeless man's shanty.

"This is it?" He asked.

"Yup," Jason said with great pride.

"Our old one was better. It was way more awesome…but ya know…" Brett told him.

They hung out in and around the fort for well over an hour. Throwing rocks, playing with a sling shot they tried to construct, and they played a quick round of black jack with a deck of cards they had stashed out there and some acorns…Lucas lost four dollars in acorns.

Finally Jason could not take the boredom any longer, "It's going to be dark soon. Let's get everyone together and play chase," he suggested.

"Yeah," Brett replied, "that's a great idea."

The three young boys put away their cards and sling shot, and closed up the 'fort'.

They climbed over the log, and stepped on each of the three stones. Brett carefully inspected the area and found no one nearby before he opened the brush passageway. As Lucas ducked through behind Jason, he noticed the brown dog sitting quietly in the woods just three feet further up the path from them. He gasped and froze. Brett passed through the small hole and covered the secret opening. He looked up the path and saw nothing, then led them out of the woods.

Lucas stood frozen, but the dog was no longer in sight. He was still present though, he could feel it. Lucas gazed back several times over his shoulder as he felt the carnivorous eyes upon him. The dog never showed himself again. *I know you're out there,* Lucas thought to himself. *Why don't you show yourself, you stupid mutt?*

When they reached the edge of the woods, Jason suggested that they divide up and get everyone. "I'll run through the Manor quick and tell everyone, and you guys get your brothers and everyone in that direction."

"Wait guys." Lucas started to sweat…*This is going to be so embarrassing he thought.* "I have to be home before dark. For dinner," he added.

"Oh. Okay, well you can play a little while can't ya'" Jason asked.

Lucas shook his head.

"Hey," Brett suggested, "why don't ya call her from my house and ask?"

"Okay." Lucas agreed and did just that. He was smart enough to play the ' but I finally made some friends,' card and his mother allowed him, just this once, to stay out after dark on a school night.

Most of the kids in the neighborhood were busy that night, but about ten showed up at the baseball field behind the Parish Hall. They broke up into teams, and set the boundaries. Beyond the woods in the back and the houses on the sides were out, and the utility green pipes at the hall were jail. Once you were caught you were sent to the green pipes, until someone from your team ran by and freed you!

The kids played for hours, well into the dark they chased each other. They would get thrown in jail, and then someone waiting nearby from the other team would dart out and touch them, setting them free again. Lucas had a wonderful time. Never had he felt like part of such a great neighborhood of kids before. Never was he so welcomed so quickly.

They played until they were too tired to run, and then they all slowly strolled home. Lucas with a giant grin on his face. He had made friends. He felt for the first time like this might be a place where he could belong.

Goin' Fishin'   5

"We're going fishing in the morning," Brett told
him with a bit more excitement. "Do you fish at
all?"

"Oh yeah," Lucas told him, "My dad and I used to
fish in Maine a lot."

"Okay, well we're goin' out pretty early."

"Where do you go?"

"We just fish off the trestle bridge," Brett told him
pointing over towards the bridge that divided the
town.

Lucas nodded as if he knew where he meant, and
then asked about the time they were leaving. Brett
shrugged his shoulders and looked over at Jason.

"Let's go in the middle of the night," Jason
suggested.

"No, my parents won't let me go then. Plus Robbie
is going, and there's no way he'll want to do that."
Brett thought about it then went into the kitchen
where Robbie was making a box of macaroni and
cheese. He reappeared a few minutes later to
announce that they would go at 5:00 am. That was
as close to the middle of the night as he would give
them.

Jason and Lucas agreed and started to move towards
the door. Lucas remembered his slingshot he had
left up in Brett's room and ran to get it as Jason

headed home on his bike. As he reappeared with his wrist rocket in hand he thought that he ought to mention that it was doubtful his mother would let him out to play that early in the morning.

"I kinda don't know that my mom is gonna go for me leaving at five am."

"Can you sneak out?" Brett asked.

"I can try. But if I get caught then I won't be able to go to the bowling party."

Brett contemplated the new predicament, "why don't you just stay here tonight?"

"Like sleep over?"

"Yeah," Brett nodded. "We'll sleep out on the screen porch…it'll be fun."

Lucas nodded in agreement. It sounded like fun. "I'll ask my mom. I'm sure she'll say yes."

"Okay, call me if you can't."

With that Lucas rode home to ask permission to spend the night at the Wilson's. After agreeing to wash the dinner dishes, Lucas was back on his bike with a backpack strapped on and his fishing pole in hand. He rode down English Road right past Jason's house wondering if Brett had called him to come over too. Then he turned once again down North Street towards the church. One more turn onto Clarey Ave and he was there. He stood the bike respectfully next to the garage and his fishing pole next to it. He was careful to not let either item be in the way at all, and then he knocked on the back door. Tommy opened the door and let the boy in. Lucas was dwarfed by Tommy's large presence. Cowering slightly, he ran quickly through the house and up to the bedroom where Brett was sitting on his bed bouncing a small rubber ball against the wall.

"So what do you wanna do?" Brett asked.

"I don't know."

"Wanna watch a movie?"

"It's still kinda early. Let's do something outside for a while," Lucas suggested.

"Like what?"

"I don't know," he shrugged.

Together they both walked back down the stairs and through the front screened porch. They sat side by side on the cement blocks as they looked around at the neighborhood. Then Brett got up off their perch and grabbed the basketball. Lucas followed. He hated playing hoops. He was the shortest kid in the whole world, which made basketball very little fun.

"Alright shortie," Brett teased him, "let's teach you some skills."

Lucas rolled his eyes as he checked the ball Brett had passed to him.

"Now I've never been short so I don't exactly know what you're going through," Brett laughed.

"You had to be short once you ass."

Brett shook his head as he dribbled a circle around the small boy, "Nope. I was born this size. They call me, *The Birdman*," and he shot a basket that was nothing but net. "You know....Larry Bird," as he grinned through his hundreds of freckles.

Brett recovered the ball and passed it once again to Lucas. "Okay. So you don't *have* to be short and useless. You can be short and ...." he thought for a moment, "wirey." He clapped his hands together once towards Lucas, then opened them up to receive the ball (everyone knows this means 'ball me.')

Lucas passed the ball and then placed himself crouched over in front of the basket with his hands on his knees, in an attempt to guard. Brett started dribbling again and began spinning himself first right and then back to the left as he dribbled. He started to move around Lucas to the left then double backed to the right, showing him how easy it could be to get by. "See it's not all about towering over the other guy. Sometimes you need to fake 'em out. And sometimes you gotta slide underneath. That'll be your job." Brett continued to prance around the court with the ball endlessly bouncing beside him. "Now, one on one...well, you're toast. But, as a team, we could be pretty good."

He told Lucas to stand in guard of the basket with his hands up. "Okay. So if you were the tall guy, and I was you," he said as he dribbled up to his opponent, "you get up close, then you fake to the left, roll right, and go underneath." Brett stopped. "Now you're not gonna make the basket, cause he's got more reach. But if you make like you're gonna with your eyes and your body," he showed him with his body facing the basket and his eyes glued to the rim. "Then you bounce pass it out to me in the wings." Brett ran out to the three point line and swished the ball through, "I shoot. We score!" The demonstration was over. "Now let's try it. Pretend there's a big guy there and you have to get by him and get the ball out to me."

Lucas could feel Brett's energy. He was excited about having a secret game plan with the basketball star. He took the orange inflatable rock and started to emulate everything Brett did. He dribbled into the imaginary giant that stood between him and his two points. He faked left. Then he rolled right. His feet got tangled....he fell. Lucas laid there on the cement court as the ball rolled away, and the sting began to come from his palms. He lifted his hands and saw the scrapes along both as the blood was starting to seep through.

"You alright?" Brett asked.

Lucas nodded, and got to his feet. "You got a rag or something I can wipe my hands off on?"

Brett took him over to the side of the garage where they ran both his hands under the spigot, then dried them on his pants. Together they went back to try the move again. Lucas did a little better the next time...or at least he didn't fall. He faked, he rolled, he passed and Brett shot. This time the ball bounced off of the rim and rebounded to Lucas.

"Okay," Brett started with a smile, "you didn't fall down," he laughed. "But you have to look at the basket with your eyes and your body while you pass the ball out to me. You know where I am, and I am staring at you. I'll catch the ball Luke, just send it my way. But don't look at me." Brett showed him the move one more time. "It's wicked important that you don't look at me if you don't have to. That way they think you're going to the rim with it and we fake them out."

Lucas nodded that he understood. *Just know where Brett is and pass it*, he thought to himself. They did the move a few more times, improving with every attempt. Finally it was too dark to see. They placed the ball by the tree and went back to the front porch.

"I'll teach ya some more tricks, and then we'll kick all their asses," Brett joked.

Lucas nodded and smiled at the idea.

"Let's go see what's on TV," Brett suggested and they went back inside. They caught reruns of Chips and Charlie's Angles, and talked about trying to stay up for Saturday Night Live, but decided they had to get up early and should try to get some shut eye.

Grabbing their blankets and pillows from Brett's room, they carried them out to the screened front porch. The sheets were draped over the chairs as a tent and then they climbed underneath with the heavy blankets and pillows. As any two young kids would do, they sat and told stories as they attempted to drift off to sleep. Interrupting their conversation, they heard a tree branch break from the side of the house. The boys went silent! They lay there listening to the night as they clearly heard footsteps coming around the side of the house! Timidly they peered through the opening in the sheet tent and over the side wall of the porch.

Together they watched as two figures moved around the front of the house and over to the Wilson's station wagon. The car door very quietly opened and one figure sat down inside behind the wheel. The other walked to the front of the car and waited. The person in the car reached up for the shifter, and put the car into neutral as the other gave it a push out of the driveway. The car quietly creaked backwards out onto Clarey Ave as the driver turned the wheels. The second figure then ran to the back and gave it a push forward towards the stop sign.

"They're stealing your dad's car!" Lucas started to move, but Brett grabbed his arm and pointed back to the grand theft auto in progress. They watched the car roll past the front of the house and the second person running alongside climbed inside. It was Dave! Dave and Tommy were stealing the station wagon! It reached the stop sign before the curious young boys heard the engine finally start up. "Whoa," was all Lucas could say.

Brett laughed out loud at his ingenious brothers. "I know how they sneak out, but I never knew that they rolled the car down the road and then drove off in it."

Lucas couldn't believe what he had just seen. Never in all his wildest dreams would he ever have come up with such a great way to go out at night.

"We better go to sleep now. If we make any noise that brings my parents down, then my brothers'll get caught."

Both boys climbed back under the sheet tent and curled up on their pillows.

Morning came quickly. Rather, five a.m. came quickly and Brett's second oldest brother Robbie was kicking both of the boys. Groggy, they wiped the sand from their eyes and peered out at the teenager eating his cereal, all the while kicking them both. The boys got to their feet as if it were just another day, then both quickly turned and looked out the screen windows. The Station Wagon was right where Mr. Wilson had left it the night before.

They dressed quickly and each grabbed a pop tart as they went out to the garage to get their fishing poles. With poles in hand and Robbie armed with the tackle box, they started down Clarey Ave towards the bridge. As they reached the stop sign, they saw Jason Sharper riding as hard as he could towards them. They waited for him in silence, and then together, they quietly walked through town. It was too early to speak. Except for a few cars driving through town; all of Hampton Mills was still fast asleep.

They did not fish from the bridge on North Street, but instead, cut into the woods alongside the Cider Mill Creek until they reached the old trestle bridge. Many years ago, the train used to run right through Hampton Mills to Stop Eight. The tracks were no longer in use and the trestle bridge was great for fishing, as well as other various mischievous activities.

They lingered around the base of the creek, where the water was both high, and flowing rapidly this time of year. They searched with their small hands for earth worms, pulling them from the ground to use as bait. Once their hooks were baited, they cast their lines into the strongly flowing green water below. There, they each sat in the quiet outdoors just watching their lines. Jason caught the first fish of the morning, but threw it back because of its small stature. Brett and Lucas both caught slightly larger fish and kept them for lunch. Robbie on the other hand, had lost three worms and was plenty frustrated. He walked back down off the bridge and searched once again along the creek bed for better bait, when he suddenly heard a strange noise. It sounded like a child crying out. It was a long bleating noise that seemed to be growing louder.

The boys each got to their feet and secured their poles as they searched for the lost or hurt child.

"Do you see anything?" Jason asked.

"Shhh…" Robbie yelled up to him with authority.

Suddenly from under the North Street Bridge they saw something in the water. It was tan, and trying desperately to keep its head above water as the current rushed it towards them. Robbie quickly pulled off his warm jacket and sneakers and dove into the cold creek water. He swam into the current that was moving this helpless victim towards them. As he got close enough to it, he wrapped his left arm around the neck and swam kicking as hard as he could to the shore. He reached the bank where he could touch the ground and stood up, now wrapping both arms around the cold, helpless being. Rising out from the water Robbie shivered with the baby deer curled in his arms. It was a small brown fawn whose spots were fading, that must have been swept from the others by the current.

Quickly the boys gathered their gear and ran to Robbie's side. Lucas grabbed Robbie's heavy coat and wrapped it around the scared little fawn. Together they carried her home. It was now around 6:30 in the morning and the people of Hampton Mills were starting to appear little by little. What a sight these four kids were walking through town with their bundled up baby deer. They reached the house on Clarey Ave and Jason opened the door to the screen porch. Robbie carried her inside and set her gently on the floor. Lucas quickly thought to run and close the door into the house so that the baby deer did not wander inside. Brett had grabbed a few towels off of the clothes line as they came through the yard and they began to dry her soft, wet fur.

"So what do we do?" Brett asked his older brother.

"Got me," Robbie laughed.

"Better get your mom and dad," Lucas chimed in.

Brett and Robbie both agreed and went to fetch their parents. Robbie quickly ducked into his room to change into dry clothing as Brett found his parents in the living room reading the morning paper.

"Mom. Dad. You guys need to come see this," he said as he motioned them out of the room. Both parents followed their youngest son through the house. As he reached the door, he turned and added, "Robbie had to rescue a baby from the creek."

"A baby!" his mother cried out.

Mr. Wilson pushed Brett aside as he opened the porch door, with Mrs. Wilson right behind him. They stopped cold in their tracks. They stood in shock as the baby fawn lay quietly on their porch floor in a bundle of blankets…and mom's handmade quilt. They spoke not one word as they gazed upon the small wonder.

Robbie came back down stairs in clean dry clothes, "so what do you think of that mom?" he asked in his high, crackling, pubescent voice.

"What happened, Robbie?" she asked.

"I don't know," he replied with raised eyebrows and excitement in his voice. "We were fishing, then we heard this thing crying, so I jumped in and saved it."

"There were no others around?" Mr. Wilson asked.

"We didn't see any," Brett answered.

"What's going on down here?" they heard Tommy from the doorway.

"Is that a baby deer?" Dave asked peering through the crowd.

Mr. Wilson took a deep contemplating breath. "Okay," he started, "you boys go back out and very quietly walk up and down the creek and look for any signs of other deer. Footprints. Something like that." He knew that the deer was too old to still need his mother, but he needed to give the boys a mission.

"Mary, why don't you see if you can get in touch with the City Zoo, maybe they'll take it in. Robbie you stay here with it. Maybe get it some milk in a bowl." Mr. Wilson started to walk away, "and if it has an 'accident' Robbie," he said with finger quotes around *accident*, "clean it up."

Everyone did as they were instructed. The boys all moved quietly up stream looking for any signs of deer. They played like they were woodsman from the north country tracking a big kill. They looked for footprints, broken tree limbs, even tree rubs from antlers. They found nothing, so they headed back to the house unsuccessful.

Mrs. Wilson had called the local zoo, and they agreed to take in the deer. Dad had gotten dressed and made room in the back of the station wagon (still sitting just as he had left it the night before) for the deer. Robbie sat quietly with the young fawn, drying her brown fur the best he could and talking gently to her. He had served her a bowl of milk that she was too frightened to drink, and she had in fact experienced a nervous 'movement' that he had to clean up….just as his dad had instructed him to do.

Mr. Wilson carefully carried the small wonder out to the wagon and placed her in the back. Robbie climbed in through the back seat and sat with his arms securely around her to hold her still on the trip. The rest of the family along with the two other young boys stood in the driveway as Mr. Wilson backed the car down the drive and left with the fawn to her new home.

"They'll take good care of her there. She'll probably have a better life then she would have out there in the woods." Mrs. Wilson offered the consoling, motherly words of wisdom as they all headed back inside.

House Hunting   6

The night had been extraordinarily long. They
finally had fallen to sleep around four am, but the
commotion in the kitchen had woken Brett from his
slumber. He scratched his red top and rubbed the
sleep from his eyes as he left Lucas alone still fast
asleep on the porch, and made his way to the
bathroom. Their parents had left early in the
morning for a day up in New Forrest with Mary
Ellen and her friend.

The commotion that Brett had heard was his two
oldest brothers wrestling for the last frozen waffle.
Tommy had won. The young boy sat down at the
table resting his head heavy in his hands. He
watched as Tommy pulled the frozen pastry from
the toaster and smothered it with syrup. He
watched Robbie reach for it once as Tommy
stabbed his hand with the fork tines, which of
course made Robbie giggle like a school girl. Then
he laid his head onto the kitchen table and closed
his eyes listening to them speak about their busy,
important lives.

"What hours are you working today?" Robbie had
asked Tommy.

"Nine to five today. Just like the song says," he
joked.

This, of course, sent Robbie into a quick chorus of
Dolly Parton's hit, "Workin' nine to five, what a
way to make a living." Then he shoved his baby
brother, "how's it go Brettie?" he asked as he
attempted to fold up his arms to create giant breasts.

Brett laughed and folded his arms up too. "Workin' nine to five…" that was really all he knew of the entire song.

Robbie had Dolly Parton danced his way over to the mud room and gazed out at the beautiful day. "I think I'll go to the mall today," he added. "pick up chicks," he said raising his eyebrows to his brothers.

"Yeah, right Robbie," Tommy doubted him.

Robbie noticed his father's hunting rifle standing in the mud room, leaning against the doorway. He reached down and placed one hand on the barrel, gesturing it towards Tommy, "You gotta ask yourself….Do you feel lucky, punk?" He had lifted the barrel of the rifle slightly off the door frame, then placed it back down again gently.

"That ain't funny Robbie," Tommy said, while laughing with syrup running down his pale chin.

Robbie turned to walk back into the kitchen, but in his slight rotation, his foot caught the butt of the gun. The rifle fell in the opposite direction. As it hit the door frame on the other side of the walk way, it exploded! The gun went off in the house!

Lucas sat straight up.

Dave who was upstairs fast asleep as well, sat straight up in his bed.

The three in the kitchen area jumped in fright, then froze in their place. All three were shaken, with their eyes the size of quarters and mouths fallen open. Brett felt himself actually trembling as he stood close to his oldest brother. Then, as if they were one unit with a shared brain; all three boys slowly moved their eyes from the smoking gun in the doorway, to the hole in the ceiling. They remained motionless, as they gazed up at it.

"DAVE!" Tommy yelled out as he ran for the stairs. Dave stood at the top of the steps in his tee shirt and shorts with his hair all a mess. "Are you alright?" Tommy asked.

"What the hell was that?"

Tommy took in a deep breath, as his brothers appeared behind him.

"Jesus Dave, are you alright?" Robbie asked, Brett still trembling at their side.

"Yeah. What the hell was that? It scared the shit outa me."

"Jesus," Robbie said again as he sat down in the arm chair with his hands covering his face.

"Robbie was messin' around with dad's gun and it went off," Tommy explained.

"NO!" Robbie argued. "I touched it kidding around. Then when I was walking away, I kicked it. It fell over and went off." He looked at Tommy with disgust, "Why ya making it sound like I was aiming it at people. Jesus."

Dave stood at the top of the stairs in disbelief. "Wait. So that was dad's gun?" he asked. "That was a gun shot in our house? Holy Crap!" he exclaimed, then marched down the stairs and through the kitchen to see the bullet hole.

Tommy, and Brett followed, but Robbie remained in the arm chair. They trudged through the house, back through the kitchen and gazed up at the hole.

"Robbie," Dave called out to him laughing, "You shot our house!"

Tommy and Brett started to snicker under their breath. "Holy crap Dave. That's right under your room," Tommy said as he rubbed his finger tips over the whole.

Dave turned his head as he studied the wound, "I think that's right under my bed!"

The three boys started laughing when Robbie reappeared at the scene of the crime. "I'm glad that you find it so hilarious that I almost killed you Dave. Idiot." He added as he sat down at the table.

"Robbie. Come on. I'm fine," Dave pointed back at the ceiling and started laughing again, "but you killed the house."

The three continued to laugh as Robbie sat confounded at what to do. "I am so dead," he stressed. "There's no way to hide that."

"Yeah we can." Brett who had been mute since the rifle exploded finally spoke. "I can spackle over that and slop some paint on it before they get home. Nobody'll even know it's there."

"Really?" Tommy asked.

Brett nodded with confidence, and proceeded downstairs to get the bucket of spackle and the putty knife. He reappeared with his supplies, and climbed up on to a kitchen chair. "You want the bullet?" he asked with a Cheshire cat grin.

"You got it?" Robbie asked excitedly with wide eyes.

Brett began to laugh as he was psyching out his older brother, "no, you dumb ass. I don't see it up here anywhere."

Robbie's face became more serious as he threatened his younger brother, "I'm gonna kick the crap out of you."

Brett started to dismount the chair, "Okay then. I'll leave the hole."

Robbie stopped him from getting all the way down, "Alright," he agreed rolling his eyes, "I'm sorry."

Brett let out a deep sigh, climbed back up and began patching the ceiling when an important fact finally dawned on Tommy, "Hey. Didn't you have a friend here last night?"

"Oh Crap!" Brett exclaimed as he leapt from the kitchen chair and all four brothers ran out to the screen porch. They open the door to find Lucas curled up in the wicker chair in the corner of the room clearly frightened.

"You alright?" Tommy asked the scared little boy.

Lucas nodded slightly, as he stared at them.

"You sure?" Dave asked. "Because Robbie's shootin' guns off and stuff," he laughed.

"Shut up jerk."

"ooooo, be vewy quiet," Dave continued to mock in an Elmer Fudd imitation, "He's hunting houses."

"You're an ass Dave," Robbie said in a huff as he stormed off of the screen porch, "I shoulda shot your dumb ass."

Brett approached his friend still curled up tight in his mom's wicker furniture and sat beside him. They were quiet. Finally Brett broke the silence, "Pretty screwed up huh?" Lucas nodded. Brett nodded along with him. "That scared the hell out of all of us." Lucas raised his brow and nodded again. "This one's a first." Lucas looked at his friend questioning if that was really the first time, given all of the other crazy stuff he had heard about or born witness to. "Come on," Brett motioned him off of the chair. "Can you help me fix the hole, so my parents don't find out?" Lucas got to his feet and followed him into the house.

Brett showed him the hole in the ceiling and climbed up onto the chair, "Can you pass me the spackle?" Lucas passed up the bucket. "See I gotta

fix it, cause none of these morons know how."
Lucas smiled as Brett scrapped over the white fill to
smooth it out. "There. Like a baby's bottom," he
smiled and climbed down from the chair.

"So now what Brett?" Robbie asked. "Mom and
Dad are gonna notice that."

"It dries Robbie." Brett rolled his eyes at the lack
of sense his brother possessed. "It dries, and I come
back here in a little while and paint over it."

"Okay," he nodded, "Thanks buddy."

"Yeah," Brett answered with disgust.

"Okay, you guys come in here," Robbie called them
all to the kitchen table. He sat at the head and
addressed his brothers along with the stray kid that
was unfortunate enough to be caught up in the mess.
"We have to all swear...*all of us*," he said looking
directly at Tommy, "to never say a word about this
ever again." They all took Robbie's plea very
seriously and agreed. He however, didn't feel that
that was quite enough. "I'm serious
now...Tommy...Luke."

"What?" Tommy protested.

"What?, Don't what me. You run to Mom about
everything."

"I do not."

"Ya kinda do," Dave agreed.

Tommy sat in anger as Robbie continued, "How about you, kid?"

Lucas sat back, almost offended by the accusation. "He's ok," Brett interrupted. "You don't have to worry about him at all."

"Okay. So no one say one word, right?"

Once again they all agreed and were excused from the table.

So, Do you like her?   7

The local youth group was holding a bowling party at the Rowing Park Bowling Alley on Saturday afternoon for all youths. The Cooper's had agreed to take a number of the boys there if the Wilson's would in turn, bring them home.

Once inside the bowling ally the party began: food and beverages, a jukebox, video games, a pool table, and of course, bowling. The girls gathered around the jukebox, hoping to find the perfect *Journey* tune to play. The boys ignored them and played video games; that is except for Jason Sharper, who leaned against the wall sipping his Mug Root Beer to appear cool and available. It was a typical boy girl event.

As the girls gathered in the corner, watching the preteen boys crowd around Space Invaders, Kimberly James finally emerged from the pack. Strutting across the floor, she approached Lucas and asked him point blank if he liked Jana.

Jana Harris had moved to J.D.W. School the year before, and was never considered shy, however at this moment, she was frantically flipping through the titles in the jukebox to appear uninterested in what Kim was doing.

When the crowd of boys overheard the inquiry, a collective "whooaaaa," came from the group followed by laughter. Lucas took in a deep breath trying to look everywhere except directly at Kim *or* Jana. He felt himself starting to sweat again. He suddenly wished it were gym class and he were being chose last for teams…that, he thought, would be less humiliating.

"Well?" Kim asked him.

Lucas glanced up at her for only a second. The *play it cool* approach had gone completely out the window. That applied to his guy friends. He had never thought of any scenarios that involved a girl before. He had never seen this coming! There was *no* preparation for this one whatsoever. He looked over at Joe Cooper who loved to try and impress the girls…he was laughing. *No help there,* Lucas thought to himself. Finally Jason stepped in, putting his arm around the shoulder of his new friend.

"I'll tell ya what Kimmie," he started. "My boy here is pretty cool. He likes to…" he slowly swayed back and forth with his head as Lucas hung on to his every word and struggled to appear cool. "Think about things," he finally added. Lucas nodded very slightly and pursed his lips in deep thought. "Why don't you give the kid some space; let him mull it over, and we'll get back to ya."

Lucas was afraid to look directly at her. He waited. Kimberly James stood with one hand on her hip as the other twirled a lock of blond hair that rested on her shoulder, all the while glaring at Jason Sharper from below raised brows with both skepticism and disgust.

"You're such an ass Jason." She spun around in her black shoes and walked back to the group of girls, shaking it for all that it was worth…she knew the boys were watching.

The boys did watch, but only for a second, before they all very coolly turned back to the arcade game and started playing again like nothing had happened.

But it had! Lucas was now sick to his stomach and his heart was pounding. *Why me?* He thought, *why did she have to pick me?*

Brain Haulk was feverishly kicking space invader butt, when he had the presence of mind to finally ask, "So Reed. *Do* you like her?"

Oh great. Now everybody wants to know. "I don't know," he shrugged. "I don't really know her."

"You don't have to *know* her," Joe piped in.

"Yeah. You just have to know if you like her," added Jason.

"What's the difference?"

"Well it's not like ya gotta marry the girl for God sakes," Jason explained excitedly. Sister Anne from the youth group overheard the blond boy's use of the Lords name in vain, and shot a dirty look in the direction of the arcade game. "Sorry ma'am," Jason responded respectfully. Then he leaned into the crowd a bit more, as Brian excitedly pounded on the 'fire' button. "You just gotta know if you wanna kiss her," and he stood back up from the group in all his glorious wisdom.

"Eewwwww….." they all teased, with a few added kiss, kiss noises.

Lucas was flush with embarrassment. He had never once thought about kissing a girl. He was still trying to make guy friends in his mind. Lucas stood over Brian's shoulder and watched, occasionally yelling out at the game. As he saw his own reflection in the glass screen of the arcade game, he wondered what this dark haired, dark eyed boy would do.

"Dude, Gimme some money."

Lucas heard a familiar voice from behind them. It was Dave Wilson shaking his little brother down for some cash.

"I don't have any money," Brett told him.

"Yeah. Ya do."

"I don't," Brett yelled back at him.

"I seen you just a minute ago, with cash out!" Dave looked around realizing that they were drawing attention, "Come on Brettie. I just want to buy this girl a pretzel."

"No," Brett whined. "I got like, two bucks left. And it's *my* money. It's all I got."

Dave leaned in close to his little red haired brother about to threaten his young life when Brett started in again, "I earned this money. I got up at the crack

78

of ass every morning and picked strawberries all summer. Not you."

Dave stood up and rolled his eyes with a calming deep breath. Glaring with disgust, he tucked his hands into his pockets and started to walk away, turning back just once to point out, "You know mom and dad wanted a girl."

Lucas walked over to Brett standing by the pool table in the middle of the rec-room, "Wow. I thought he was gonna kick your butt," he said.

"So did I," Brett laughed. "Come on, let's play some Paper Boy."

The two boys walked over to the video game and dropped in their quarters to rack up points while they hazardously delivered the newspaper. "So do you like her?" Brett asked. "Shut up," Lucas replied with a playful shove.

"Do ya?" he asked again through his laughter.

"Get outa here."

"That's a good idea." A new ominous voice.

Two figures towered over them casting a shadow across their paper route. Lucas turned to see two seventh graders who also lived in Hampton Mills. Jim Woodcock was an average sized kid with ratty brown hair and was always seen in a white tee shirt and parachute pants. He and his friend, everyone only knew as Porker, because of his stocky build, were from the other side of the bridge. He turned back to the game and continued to play, when he felt a two finger jab in his left shoulder. Lucas glared back at him, but was not brave enough to speak. He continued to play. He was jabbed again, only this time it was more of a shove. Brett pulled both hands off the game and spun around in his Pony's to confront them.

"What's your problem man?" he asked while his blue eyes stared down his opponent.

"You."

Brett raised his eyebrows and shrugged his shoulders as if to say, 'that's your problem.'

"This is my game," Jim Woodcock informed him.

Brett stared at him a second longer then turned back to the arcade game. He began searching the machine. He looked at the screen, he squatted down to the front of it, then looked to the sides, and finally leaned back to look at the very top, "I don't see your name on it."

The kid moved in closer and put his hand on Brett's shoulder, as the other bully moved in to Lucas and stared him down in silence. "Oh, you're a real funny one, aren't you," he said to Brett through clenched jaw.

Brett stood his ground. He had taken beatings from far bigger kids then this punk. Lucas on the other hand, thought he was going to pee. Then from out of nowhere, he found himself hoping that Jana Harris wasn't watching.

"There a problem here?" someone asked from behind the two seventh graders.

"Yeah. Mind your own business," the kid told the person without flinching.

The third party hesitated for only a split second before he grabbed the kid by the neck and placed him firmly against the wall. It was Dave Wilson again. He had come to his brother's aid. Porker watched as Dave held his friend against the orange paint and instructed him to leave the boys alone. Then he released his grip and watched them both leave the game area and go back to the lanes. Dave silently looked at his little brother, and his little brother at him. Although no words were spoken, there was an understanding between the two of them. One was asking, 'You alright?' and the other was replying, 'Yeah, thanks.' Then Dave walked back to the girl at the snack bar.

Lucas watched the unspoken bond between brothers, then suddenly remembered that Jana Harris was still somewhere in the bowling ally. *Had she seen it?* he wondered. *Had she seen me not back down? Oh my god! What do I care if she saw all of that? What is happening to me? Stupid Kim.*

The boys went back to their game. But something troubled Lucas about the previous events. "You know what I don't get? Dave was mad at you. I mean I thought he was gonna lay you across that pool table, but then he walked away…I mean that part I understand. But then a few minutes later, he defends you against those two jerks."

"Yeah?" Brett asked.

"Well why didn't he just let them pound you?"

"He's my brother," Brett answered casually.

"That's the way brothers go," Jason Sharper chimed in from over their shoulders. "See they can beat the snot out of ya. Smack ya, kick ya, pants you in front of the whole school…but anybody else dares to mess with ya, they got another thing comin'," Jason explained.

Lucas nodded his head as if he understood.

"You really got no brothers or sisters Lucas I Can't REED?" he asked.

"I read better then you candy ass." Lucas pulled at the strings on his hooded sweatshirt. "It's just me and my mom most of the time."

"Where's your dad?" Jason asked.

Lucas shrugged his shoulders, "Korea right now."

"Korea? What's he do, make toys?" Jason joked.

Lucas laughed, "no, he's stationed there for a month, then he comes home around Christmas. But then he has to leave the day after Christmas for Europe, for some stupid thing that's gonna keep him there for like three or four months I guess."

"Wow. That sucks," Brett said, and the conversation was over.

He got through the rest of the party without having anyone else bring up what he would refer to as *the Jana situation* again, and he managed to steer clear of her and Kimberly James with her questions. Mr. Wilson arrived to chauffeur the group home and the gang of boys filed out of the building. Lucas was last at the shoe rental counter, but Mr. Wilson promised that he would not leave without him. He turned in his shoes, and made for the door. As he reached for the knob, so did another hand; Jana Harris! She and her mom were on their way out as well. They both pulled back their hands and smiled averting their eyes. Then, as if channeling Isaac Washington straight off the *Love Boat*, he mustered up all of his courage and coolness, and he did as gentleman do. Lucas Reed reached up and opened the door, holding it for both ladies to pass. Then he threw up a little bit in his mouth. They thanked him and he politely smiled before running to the station wagon.

Dave had called shot gun, while Robbie rode in the back seat behind his dad. Joe and Paul Cooper sat in the seat next to Robbie while Jason and Brian waited in the backend for Lucas. In all his embarrassment Lucas quickly scurried over the tailgate and pulled the window shut behind him.

"Hey Luke. Is that Jana I just saw you walking out with?" Brian asked.

Lucas tried to ignore him as he got into position next to Jason.

"Were you walkin' behind her so you could check out her…" Jason looked up front to Mr. Wilson in the rearview mirror, then mouthed the word *Ass* as he made grabbing, squeezing motions with his hands.

"Shut up Sharper," Lucas dismissed him.

"Luke and Jana sittin' in a tree…" he laughed, gesturing to Brian to sing along. He suddenly felt a hand come from over the seat and smack the side of his head.

"Shut up Sharper," Robbie instructed him.

Lucas stared at his Reeboks and thought about his afternoon. A girl that likes him, an almost fight, and now teased in the back of the station wagon. Then he looked around the car at the others wondering what they thought of Jana and the other girls…or did they ever think of girls…or did they…wait. Lucas leaned over the backseat towards the adult behind the wheel, "Mr. Wilson. Where's Brett?"

Mr. Wilson glanced up to the rearview mirror and took a head count as he sped down Rikland Ave. Then he pulled into a driveway and turned the car around.

The History Lesson
in The Mess Hall   8

Lucas tossed restlessly on the floor of Brett's room while Brett himself lay silent and peaceful in his bed. Frustrated by his boredom he decided to use the bathroom, *at least that was something to do.* He snuck very quietly down the hall careful not to wake anyone, and closed the door behind him. He lifted the lid and proceeded to spell out his name in the crystal blue water. Dropping the lid back down, he flushed and washed his hands. *Jees*, he thought. *I could use a drink.* He reached for the cup holder mounted on the wall next to the vanity mirror, but found it empty. He contemplated briefly and decided that he could quietly sneak downstairs to get some water.

Lucas once again snuck as silently as he could down the hallway. He tiptoed past Mr. and Mrs. Wilson's room to the stairs and slowly crept down. In his mind he was a special agent on a top secret government mission. He stepped in very specific spots on each step, just as Brett had taught him, careful not to make them creak, and he double checked around every corner. As he rounded the last corner to the kitchen, he spotted a figure at the table. He pulled back and stood up straight and tense, hidden behind the wall. He looked once more and saw Tommy sitting at the table gazing up at the corner cupboard. *Damn. How will I get past this patrol?*

In this game, Lucas made believe that Tommy Wilson was an enemy guard patrolling the 'Mess

Hall.' He took one step back causing his foot to lightly kick the wall. He gasped with his hand over his own mouth and froze. He waited a short moment then peered around the corner once more. Tommy was starring back at him. *How stupid I must look lingering back here.* Lucas felt like a fool. *I'm the worse spy ever in the history of the world.* He stepped out into plain sight, trying not to look directly at the big senior and headed for the cupboard.

"Hey," Tommy said to him as he sat back in the chair.

Lucas gave the chin upward gesture and smiled slightly as he reached for the cabinet door. He pulled down a plastic cup and filled it with water from the tap. Tommy sighed heavily, and looked at the small boy. "Couldn't sleep?" he asked. Lucas nodded, once again without eye contact. Tommy nodded along with him, "Yeah. Me neither." Tommy looked at the small kid again and continued to bend his ear, "If I don't pass this history test on Monday, I can't play basketball." Lucas remained in place, leaning against the kitchen sink, now looking back at Tommy. Tommy sat upright with a bit more excitement in his voice, "Hey, ya wanna help me?"

Lucas looked over the rim of his cup as he sipped, swallowed, and replied, "I'm in fifth grade."

Tommy laughed, "I know. But at the end of the chapters they have questions to quiz yourself. You can ask me the questions. Unless, you know, you wanna go back to bed."

Lucas contemplated the idea. *History's my thing. But what if I don't know this stuff and look stupid.* He was scared of Tommy; that much he knew. He cringed at the idea of possibly causing him to get kicked off the basketball team. Regardless of his fears, he sat down at the table, and Tommy handed him the textbook. He read the first question to himself. He had never actually spoken to Tommy before this night...he tried to form the words in his mouth and push them out.

"Whe," he grabbed the cup and took another swig. "What was the date of the attack on Pearl Harbor?"

Tommy sat back in the kitchen chair and crossed his arms. Sighing again heavily he proclaimed, "I know this one." He looked up at the ceiling and concentrated on a knot in the wooden beam.

"It was the 'Day that would live in infamy'," Lucas told him trying to help.

"I know. 'I fear we have woken a sleeping giant.' I know. I've seen Tora, Tora, Tora." He said, "I've seen the movie."

"It wasn't a movie. It was the greatest war in the history of the world," Lucas corrected him passionately, and then quickly checked himself. What was he doing? Why was he challenging *this* giant?

"Okay. Give me some dates...I know this."

Lucas thought of random dates and then gave him multiple answers to choose from. "February fourteenth. July Fourth. September fifth, or December seventh."

"December," he called out.

Lucas nodded. "Okay. Who killed Hitler?"

Tommy furrowed his brow in a way that made Lucas think they might actually touch, as he thought carefully about who the murderer was. "Wait," he finally said sitting tall in the chair once again. "Hitler killed himself. They think anyways."

Lucas smiled and nodded. Taking a deep breath, he continued, "It says here, to write a short essay explaining what 'D Day' was." He looked up at the man across the table, "why don't you just gimme the important facts."

Tommy sat back again and began, "'D Day' was what they called the big invasion, through France. I mean Normandy. Most of the troops landed on Omaha beach were they sustained heavy enemy fire and many lives were lost. They came by boats and they parachuted in."

Lucas smiled bigger this time, "cool." Then he thought about what 'D Day' was like for those young men, "can you imagine what that was like? Being like eighteen and riding across the ocean to fight." Lucas pictured himself as a soldier decked out in his green camouflage. His helmet sitting loosely on his head and a gun gripped tightly in his hands, while he tried to draw Tommy into the battle. He crouched over as if he were on one of the boats, scrunching his face as the chilling water splashed him and he prepared his weapon. "As soon as you get close to shore, the stupid Germans start shooting at you."

"I know," Tommy said while still uninvolved.

"And I mean, how does your luck suck so bad, that you get to sit in the first seat? As soon as the door to the boat opens, bang! You're dead. Then the rest of the guys, *your buddies*, use your pathetic body as a shield. Then once they're on shore, they toss ya on the beach and run like hell."

Tommy was surprised by the ten year olds interest in the war as he listened to him place both of them on the Normandy beach.

Lucas however, suddenly realized that he was rambling. He checked himself once again and got back on point, "Sorry. Who was the leader of Italy that aligned with Hitler in WWII?"

"Mussolini."

The two went on for well over two hours, as the young historian asked the questions and explained the answers, occasionally breaking into a full conversation about the war. Tommy had never actually viewed the 'great war' in such a way. Until that night history had just been a class to take…but this kid, he had turned it into an adventure. As for Lucas; he was in his element, and surprisingly, he found himself no longer afraid of the six foot four, varsity letter man.

Late Monday morning Tommy sat down in Mr. Lamb's History Class to take his test. As he answered each question he thought of the young boy explaining World War II to him in such detail.

Across the school yard however that same young boy was struggling with the present. Today for recess, the *cool* kids were playing basketball. Lucas' skills were improving, but he still didn't think he was ready for a game. Instead he walked off with Neil Norton and Steve Lowell, who also didn't feel much like a game of hoops. The three ventured over to the big cement tunnels and climbed on top.

They spent a good part of their half hour climbing around the tunnels and the monkey bars casually talking about absolutely nothing. Lucas had wandered by himself to the inside of one of the cement tunnels. He heard a faint noise from behind him. Turning around quickly he saw Kimberly James standing in the opening. *Oh crap.* Kim climbed inside and sat down in the curve of the passageway. She said nothing initially, so Lucas thought maybe he could keep moving and ultimately avoid the conversation. He was wrong. As he moved toward the other end, she called out his name in her sweet young voice, "Lucas."

"*Ug,*" he sighed and slowly turned back around. Certain that this wouldn't take long, he refused to sit, and instead he stood hunched over trapped inside of the cement tomb.

Kim smiled at him playfully then patted the cold hard seat next to her. Lucas took a deep breath, staring at the spot right next to her Jordache jeans. Then he leaned against the tunnel facing her instead and slid down the wall.

"So?" she asked.

Lucas shrugged and looked away as if he had no idea what she was talking about.

"Have you thought about it?"

Thought about it? How could I not? But Lucas had to be cool, (and pray that Steve and Neil would save him...quickly.) "Thought about what Kimmie?" he asked playing dumb.

Kim tilted her head in disappointment. Disappointment, and in a way that let Lucas know that she knew better. "Jana," she reminded him.

"Oh," he suddenly recalled. "Yeah. I guess I've thought about it,"

Kim waited but Lucas added nothing more. "And?"

"Oh. Um," Lucas looked around again frantically, *what do I say,* he begged internally for the answer.

"You don't like her do you?" Kim's tone had changed. She didn't sound much like a concerned friend any longer, but instead she sounded much like a girl with her own devious agenda.

Lucas shrugged again, but felt the mood in the tunnel shift greatly. For a brief moment he felt more at ease. He had this sudden recognition that something underhanded was happening and his inner secret agent kicked in. *Play it cool,* he reminded himself.

Kimberly James had moved slowly and almost unnoticeably in the tunnel and placed herself next to him; right next to him. "You know," she started, "I never really noticed you before. But I've been watching you lately."

Lucas shifted in his seat, as it occurred to him that this situation was becoming increasingly worse. But he remained composed.

"I can understand if you don't like Jana. I mean in 'that way'," she quickly added to defend herself against a possible misinterpretation. "She's fun ya know? She's my best friend! But you can't help it if you don't *like her*, like her. Ya know?" Kim pulled her comb from her back pocket and ran it softly through her feathered blonde hair. Placing her hand on Lucas' knee she added, "but we can hang out. If you wanna." She got to her hands and knees and crawled out of the tunnel without Lucas ever saying a word. She stood upright leaving Lucas' only view of her being from the waist down. She slid her pink comb back into her rear, horse encrusted pocket, and walked away. Lucas tossed his head back against the cement tunnel as he finally exhaled.

As he sat there sorting through the mess that his life had become, an upside down face appeared at the back tunnel opening. Neil and Steve had been sitting over top of them trying to listen. "Ladies man, huh?" Neil asked. Lucas rolled his eyes, *great, now everyone knows about this too.*

Recess was ending so Lucas moved out of the tunnel as Neil and Steve slid down off the topside. They walked across the black top towards the door, where Kim stood waiting before she went inside. She was hoping to catch Lucas one more time to, *steal a moment.* Instead, Lucas buried his head, as Neil pointed to him and made eyebrows to Kim. Kim rolled her eyes and spun around to find Jana standing with her arms folded across her chest. Unsure what to do, Kimberly James strutted quickly around Jana and darted back to class.

Lucas finally looked up and caught the green eyes of Jana Harris looking back at him. He wanted to look away. *If you can't see her, she can't see you,* he reassured himself. But instead of averting his eyes, *again,* he found himself smiling at her with regret. He felt sorry for her. Sorry that her friend had betrayed her in such a way. Sorry that he had left her hanging all that time. And sorry that she had possibly been misinformed, because he wasn't man enough to just go talk to her. He looked away and walked to History class.

He sat down and opened his book to the chapter on the Revolutionary war. His mind drifted briefly to Tommy Wilson. He wondered how he had made out on his test, and silently hoped he had aced it. He listened as Mr. Rockwell explained the hidden approach of the Militia versus the row marching of the Red Coats. He knew this stuff. He had seen a million reenactments, and quickly found his mind wandering. He read the Garfield poster again above the chalk board.

FOR EVERY ACTION THERE IS AN EQUAL
AND OPPOSITE REACTION.

Then Lucas spotted Kimberly James looking at him over her shoulder. He stared at her for only a moment, then tried to inconspicuously look over to Jana. Jana sat with her pencil in ready position, but watching Kim. Lucas compared the two fifth grade girls in his head. Neither one of them was really any better looking than the other was, and they both definitely had their individual points. Kim was girlie. She had pretty blonde hair that she always tended to and was starting to wear makeup and a training bra, although it was not really required.

Jana had curly brown hair with emerald eyes, but she wasn't as 'girlie' as Kim. Lucas thought of her as funny, and outgoing…usually. He thought back to his first day at J.D.W. Elementary. Neil had done something to Jana in gym class, so in return she backed him into a corner, stuck her butt out towards him, and farted loudly. Lucas found himself snickering about it even now.

"Something you want to share, Mr. Reed?" His teacher asked.

Lucas shook his head, "Sorry sir." He looked over directly at Jana as if she knew why he was laughing and smiled. Bringing his attention back around to the chalk board, Donald Stein caught his eye. Lucas didn't really know Don very well, but what he did know of him, was that he thought himself to be cool; which seamed ironic to Lucas at this very moment. He caught Don tilting his chin down towards his shoulder as he tried to shield his nose…where he was presently digging for gold. Lucas observed as he almost lost his entire finger inside of his right nostril, bend his finger to get the nail right into the wall, and finally drag out a crusty yellow bugger. Lucas gagged as he watched him inspect his jackpot carefully. He rolled it for a second between his thumb and index finger and then flicked it across the room.

On Wednesday afternoon, Tommy Wilson came home from school to find Brett and his friends already playing ping pong in their garage. He and Robbie stepped out of the old blue car and made their way to the house when Tommy noticed the backpacks by the cement steps.

"Robbie. You know which one of these it Luke's?" he asked.

"No," he answered. "I think that Blue one there," he decided pointing to the blue pile. "What are you gonna do? Swipe a beer and stuff it in there, so he gets caught?" Robbie laughed.

Tommy laughed too, and corrected him, "No. Cigarettes," he said patting his coat breast pocket.

Robbie entered the house, as Tommy squatted down to the blue pack. He unzipped the top and pulled the papers apart looking for a name. *Luke Reed*, he saw scribbled across the top of one. Next he removed something from his coat pocket and placed it inside.

Later that evening Lucas sat down at his desk and pulled his school work from the bag. Something unfamiliar to him fell out onto the pressed wood desk top. Lucas picked up the folded papers, and read the name at the top. Then his eyes moved across the page to the eighty four written in red in the top right corner of the test paper. Lucas sat down into his chair and smiled with pride.

Be A Man   9

By Thursday Lucas had all but disappeared from
existence. He had worked so hard at avoiding the
love triangle he had found himself in the middle of,
that people began to wonder if maybe he had moved
away. That evening Dave Wilson was strolling
through the Manor on his way home from his
friend's house. As he rounded the curve in the road,
he spotted a familiar face on the front porch of the
gray house. He found Lucas sitting by himself;
head heavy in his hands. In no particular hurry,
Dave approached the young boy to make sure that
everything was alright.

"Hey," he said as he approached the house.

Lucas looked up and sat back crossing his arms in
front of him.

"You okay?"

Lucas nodded, but said nothing. Dave took a seat
on the porch steps and stared out at the road. He
waited as he gave the boy a chance to open up on
his own. Lucas said nothing.

"So what's goin' on?"

Lucas pursed his lips and shook his head,
"Nothing.'"

"Did you and Brett get in a fight or something?"

"No!" Lucas corrected him quickly.

"Then why are you sittin' here all down in the dumps? Usually you're at our house causin' trouble."

Lucas still had no response.

"Ohhhh….you're grounded."

Lucas shook his head again. Finally he decided to go for it. His dad was still overseas in Korea and he needed advice. Maybe, he figured, Dave might have some insight. "Its girls," he admitted.

"Girls!" Dave sat back somewhat shocked. "I don't understand. What about em'?" he laughed.

"I don't know. It's kinda messed up."

"Whada'ya mean?"

Lucas turned himself on the steps and leaned back against the black iron railing, so that he could face the teenager. "Well," Lucas started, "Kim asked me, *in front of everyone,* if I liked this girl, Jana Harris."

"At the bowling thing, right?"

"Yeah." Lucas confirmed. Dave had some idea at least about how this all started. "Well, Jason told her I would think about it. Then Kim cornered me in the tunnel on the playground and asked me again. When I didn't say anything, she told me that it was okay not to like Jana, because *she* liked me."

"Kim?"

"Yeah. And now they're fighting. And I...I don't know what to do."

"Well," Dave started slowly to try and help the ten year old Romeo. "Which one do you like?"

Lucas shrugged.

"So you don't like one more than the other?" Dave asked.

"Not really. I mean, I don't really know either of them."

"Well, what's your gut tell ya?"

Lucas laughed, "To throw up. And maybe ask to transfer to catholic school."

Dave laughed, "No man. Girls are way more trouble there. Trust me."

"So what do I do?"

Dave pondered his predicament then turned to Lucas and asked him a question, "Chocolate or vanilla?"

"What?"

"Chocolate or vanilla?" he asked again. "Come on, don't think. Just answer fast. Chocolate or vanilla?"

"Chocolate."

"Summer or winter?"

"Winter," Lucas answered confused.

"Hot dogs or Hamburgers?

"Dogs."

"Jana or Kim?"

"Jana." Lucas caught himself off guard! Gasping, he sat up quickly with wide eyes. *Oh my God.*

Dave smiled at the dark haired kid beside him, "So I guess now we know."

Lucas nodded gently, as he wondered whether or not that was truly his decision. "So now what?" he asked.

"Whada'ya mean?"

"Now what?" he asked again. "What do I do?"

Dave shrugged his shoulders, "Ya tell her."

Lucas reached his arm around his belly as it started churning again. "So, what? I send Brett or somebody over to tell her I like her? What if she doesn't like me anymore?"

"No, no, no," Dave stopped him right there. "First of all, don't ever send someone else to talk to a girl for ya. Ever. Be a man."

That idea made him even more sick. *How in the heck do I approach a girl*, he wondered. *They travel in herds. I'll have to cut her from the herd just to talk to her.*

"Here's what you do," Dave explained. "You have to catch her alone. Somehow, you gotta get her alone. Go to the bathroom the same time she does, or get behind her in the lunch line and tell her to meet you somewhere." Dave cleared his throat and continued. "Then when you see her, you start with your apology. You tell her you're sorry for not getting back to her sooner. Period. No reason, no excuses, just that you're sorry. Then you tell her that...Kim?" he asked, as he had forgotten the other girls name already. Lucas nodded. "You tell her that Kim cornered you and never gave you a chance to speak...and before you knew it she was hitting on you."

Lucas hung on every single word that fell from Dave Wilson's mouth. "But what if she doesn't like me anymore?"

Dave thought for a moment before offering up the best way to handle that particular situation. "You're gonna have to feel that part out. If she doesn't give you anything; like she's not letting you know if she does or doesn't like you, then you might just have to throw it out there. Just be like, 'so I just wanted you to know...in case you wanted to still hang out sometime.' If she says yes, then you get her phone number. If she tells you to go to hell, then you just stay cool, and say, 'that's cool then. I just wanted set things straight between us.' Then you walk away with your head held high."

Dave felt confident that that was the best way for this kid to go. Then he added, "of course then you go into the bathroom and flip out because you just got rejected…but *never* let her see that."

Lucas smiled, as he could relate to the private freak out moments. Then he remembered the third side of the triangle, "What about Kim?"

Dave shrugged her off, "Who cares? She betrayed her friend. And you don't owe her anything."

Lucas liked that answer best, *I don't owe her anything*, he repeated to himself.

"So you all set?" Dave asked.

Lucas nodded his head and smiled, "Yeah. Until I have to actually talk to her," he laughed. "Thanks Dave."

Dave smiled at the boy and stood up from the porch. "You comin' over or what?"

"Yeah." Lucas got up as well. He had made a decision and had a feasible plan. He felt alright to move forward with his life. He yelled into his mother that he was leaving and walked with Dave through the Manor and ventured back over to Clarey Ave.

Shut Up Phil   10

The next morning Lucas awoke to the rhythmic
sound of Phil Collins singing 'Against all Odds'
loudly in his ear. *Perfect,* he thought. He
showered, dressed, and finally boarded the school
bus, all be it unwillingly. *Okay,* he thought as he sat
in the giant green seat, *It's Friday. No matter what,
I have to do this. And no one remembers what
happens on a Friday,* he tried to comfort himself. *I
can make a complete jerk of myself and by Monday,
no one will remember...I hope.*

He played it cool as the bus made each stop and the
grade school kids boarded. He kidded with Brett
and Jason as if nothing else were on his mind. Then
went up to talk to Joe and Paul about the Indiana
Jones movie they had planned to see the next day.

The beginning of the school day was like all the
others. They gathered in the hallway before the first
bell, then they filed into their rooms and said the
Pledge of Allegiance. They took their seats and
opened their math books to continue their lesson on
fractions.

Lucas sat quiet through lunch as he dreaded the
rapidly approaching recess. *Be a man,* he kept
telling himself. He threw his brown bag into the
receptacle as he slowly moved towards the back
door. It had begun to snow in Upstate New York,
so the kids each stopped at their lockers to put on
the proper boots and hat attire. Lucas shoved his
foot down into his silver and black moon boots that
his mother insisted he would need that day. *An inch
of freakin' snow, and she's got me dressed for the*

Blizzard of seventy six, he complained to himself. He capped the look off with a knit ski hat that matched his gloves, and continued on.

Today there was no plan for recess. There was no set up for dodge ball or basketball, or even a game of tag. Today was the first real snow, and the only plan was to huddle together and decide what to do with it. The group of fifth grade boys stood under the jungle gym, and just 'hung out.' *Great,* Lucas thought, *the one day that I really needed them to be busy.*

Lucas looked around. There she was. Jana Harris stood with her group of friends gathered around the swings. He watched as the white snow landed on the frayed curly ends of her braids that poked out from under her hat. He was overwhelmed with intimidation as the group of girls laughed loudly at random conversation. They were a close knit group. A tight herd. Lucas dug down deep and finally made a decision…it was now or never! He pulled his hat down around his ears, and marched away from the group with determination. With 'Against All Odds' playing on a loop in his head, Phil Collins was almost deafening to his own thoughts. As he passed by Jason Sharper, he overheard him talking to Michelle Remarc and Carrie Warbelle.

"So I got these for you guys. I figured you could put it on and kiss me," he heard Jason say to both girls as he held up two tubes of lipstick.

"Jason, you like, bought us lipstick?" Carrie asked.

Lucas slowed his steps and finally stopped, to see how this would play out.

Jason shook his head, "Heck no. I ain't no sissy. I took em' from my mom's purse."

"Jason, you're like, such a jerk," Michelle told him and both girls walked away.

And this is who I get my advice from. Lucas shook his head and rolled his eyes as he put himself back into motion. Jason spotted the small boy and quickly identified his target. Breaking into a run, he reached Lucas quickly and grabbed him from behind.

"What are you doin' man?"

"I'm *bein'* a man."

Jason looked perplexed, "What the hell does that mean?"

Lucas pointed to the group of girls. "I'm gonna cut her from the herd, and tell her that I'm sorry and that I like her."

The rest of the fifth grade boys had hurried to join in on the conversation. "Which one," Lucas heard from behind him. He stood quiet. Telling them could be bad. It could confuse what he had already worked out with Dave. "Jana." *It leaked out.*

"Jana? Really?" Neil asked.

"Dude! Kim!" Jason exclaimed. "She'll kiss ya for sure," he added waving the lipsticks around. "And I would bet anything," he paused and looked around at the rest of the guys, "you get to see her bra."

They all broke into laugher. Lucas considered the possibility. Then it occurred to him, *what the heck do I do when I see that? And kissing? Oh my God, that now too?* He shook his head. "I'm doin' this," he declared. The snow was now coming down much harder and fell in a slanting direction from the sky. Lucas pulled at his gloves, tilted his head down against the pelting flakes, and walked away from the pack. His Phil Collins theme song once again blaring in his head; *'There's so much I need to say to you. So many reasons why...'*

"It's suicide man!" he heard from behind him. "Nobody goes in there alone!" But the ex-Genesis drummer was drowning them out. Phil sang loud and clear, and spoke directly to him. Lucas kept walking. He finally reached the group of girls. Kim had seen him coming and moved herself to the outside of the group ready to receive him. The rest of the fifth grade girls turned to see this brave lone wolf approaching with no back up. Jana stood her ground. The bell rang. Recess was over.

With the wind and snow beating down even more relentlessly, they all ran for the door. Lucas stood there alone by the swings. He tried to make eye contact with Jana before she darted away, but it was brief. Kim, who had never taken her eyes off of him, worried more about her hair in the wet snow and ran off in a dash.

The song continued to play its ironic lyrics, *'So take a look at me now. There's just an empty space. And nothing left here to remind me, just a memory of her face.'* Shut up Phil!!

Lucas hung his head and slowly walked into the school. He pulled off his moon boots, and with each one came a sock. He sat down on the hallway floor to retrieve them from the insulated liner, and found himself sitting in a small puddle of muddy water. He shook his head in disgust. Pulling his socks back onto his feet and then tying his sneakers, he closed his locker and found his desk. He had failed. He never even bothered to look for Jana once inside…what was the point.

Mr. Rockwell rolled in the TV/VCR cart. "Today class, we are going to view a new movie about a famous composer. How many of you have ever heard of Mozart?" Most of the class raised their hand into the air, as he went on about what a brilliant composer this man was. Then he turned off the lights to the room, and the class watched *Amadeus*.

By one thirty, the snow and wind had heightened into a full fledged storm. Mr. Hill came over the loud speaker and announced that school was ending early and for teachers to get their students to the buses immediately. The whole school let out a cheer at the principle's words, as they all raced into the hallway to suit up for the big storm. Moon boots and hats back on, they formed their lines and pushed through the long hallway with the heavy clomping of boots rhythmically against the floor.

Lucas was about five people back from Jana Harris. He watched the back of her curled auburn head as they passed the art room, the nurse's office and the supply closet. *Quick and painless,* he told himself - *Like a Band Aid.* With a deep breath he scooted through the rest of the class and walked right up to Jana. Not caring who could hear him anymore, he started speaking. "Jana. Hey," he started. Jana was surprised, and found herself wondering how many people were watching them at that moment. Kim, two people behind, watched furiously. "So. I just wanted to say that I'm sorry," he said with great confidence. Jana did not look happy about any of this. *Sorry about what, you dumb ass!* "That I never, ya know. Let ya know. Like what I thought of Kim's question," his confidence was fading fast. "At the bowling alley," *what are you saying you gigantic ass!*

Jana nodded in recognition, but still wasn't sure where all of this was leading.

Be cool. "Anyway. I just wanted you to know. I'm sorry about that." *What else?* He tried desperately to remember everything Dave had told him. "And I never said I *didn't* like you." He motioned with his thumb behind them towards Kim. They were at the Buses. Jana nodded and started to walk away without saying a word. Out of nowhere Lucas found himself grabbing her hand. Shocked by his own actions, he very quickly realized that this was it…he was committed now. He proceeded confidently, "Look. I just wanted you to know that I'm sorry. I should have talked to you sooner. And Kim. I don't like her…she hit on me. I just wanted you to know." He let go of her hand and added, "in case you wanted to hang out some time." *Breath.*

Jana smiled at him and nodded, as the snow whipped across her face. Then still without a word, she boarded her bus.

Lucas felt good about that. *I did it. I'm a man!* He thought with great esteem. He turned with his head high and walked straight into the snow storm towards his bus. He never felt the wind or snow as it relentlessly pummeled his small body.

On a day when they are sent home early, the buses are usually very full. No one stays after for detention or extra credit help. No one is picked up early by their parents. Lucas had taken so long getting to the bus that most of the seats were already taken by the time he boarded. He looked around for an empty seat, *oh please let there be a seat with someone cool,* he thought to himself. There was nothing. Finally he pushed in next to a freckled faced second grader.

"Hey," he said as he took his seat.

"Hey," he heard confidently in return.

The kid stared at him.

"What's up?" Lucas asked with the universal chin up motion.

"What's up?"

Okay... he thought to himself as he looked sideways at the kid with raised eyebrows.

"Hey Joe," Lucas called up to Joe Cooper a few seats ahead of him.

"Hey Joe," came from his right side.

Lucas whipped his head around and glared at the kid who sat motionless on his hands with his eyes fixated straight ahead.

He turned forward again, "Joe," he repeated.

"Joe."

Lucas glared at the second grader again with a look sure to kill him.

A little girl pushed through the aisle way as she was the last one on the bus, bumping into Lucas, apologizing to him as she continued on.

"That's okay," he told her.

"That's okay."

Lucas took a deep irritated breath as he turned again towards this pain in the neck other wise disguised as a nice kid, "Really?" he asked.

"Really?"

"You got to be kidding me," he whispered under his breath, shaking his head in disgust.

"You got to be kidding me," the kid whispered as well.

"Knock it off."

"Knock it off."

"SHUT UP," he yelled at the kid.

"SHUT UP," he too yelled.

Lucas sat quiet afraid to speak. *How does this happen*, he wondered. *I'm in fifth grade...practically a man...heck I am a man. I just talked to a girl...and I can't speak now because of this little punk?*

He waited a few minutes hoping that maybe the small kid would loose interest in the irritating game. Turning in his seat so that his back was practically to the young boy, he attempted to speak again. He leaned up to Christina sitting one row up and across the aisle way, "Hey, will you switch with me?" he asked quietly trying not to be heard.

"Hey, will you switch with me," he heard quietly from beside him.

That was it! Lucas turned around in a fit of rage. He grabbed the boy by his shirt and pushed him back into the cold, metal side of the school bus as he cocked back his clenched right fist. The small second grader cringed his tiny freckled face as he braced for the punch. Lucas stopped. *What am I doing?* He thought. *What kinda man beats up a second grader?* He lowered his hand and loosened up on the kid's shirt. Glaring deep into the hazel eyes of the frightened boy, he hoped that if he pierced them enough he would get the message. Lucas sat back up and straightened out his own clothes turning back around as he tried to bury his anger.

Joe Cooper turned back and yelled something to Lucas that he could not understand.

"What?" he asked.

"What." He heard from beside him.

Oh my God, he thought. He turned again to the kid and faced him calmly. "Seriously kid. What's it gonna take?" he asked.

"Seriously kid. What's it gonna take?"

Lucas clenched his jaw. "You know I could have just railed you a second ago…but I didn't."

"You know I could have just railed you a second ago…but I didn't," the little boy repeated word for word over what Lucas was trying to say almost confusing him.

"Please!" he begged.

Silence. The little boy did not repeat this time.

"Please stop," he pleaded with despair.

Once again Silence. Lucas was dumbstruck. *Tell me it's that easy*, he thought. Afraid to push this situation, he turned back around and stared straight ahead. He would talk to no one else on this bus ride. He had had enough.

Fire and ~~Ice~~ *Mailboxes?*
11

Christmas Vacation was upon them. They were
freed from J.D.W. Elementary to live their lives.
They were boys on the loose in Hampton Mills…at
least that was the plan. The storms had hit central
NY on and off for days. School was closed both
Monday and Tuesday that week, and vacation had
begun on Wednesday.

Lucas begged his mother into letting him stay over
at the Wilson's so he and Brett could play while
there was no school. The boys sat in the living
room watching Ghostbusters for the fourteenth time
laughing at the little guy in the movie being killed
by the gargoyle as no one in the restaurant would
help him. The Wilson family had a warm fire
burning in the large stone fireplace, and Mr. Wilson
had joined them with a stack of cardboard he
planned to burn. He sat on the hearth and watched
along with his son and his friends as he carefully
placed each torn piece of box into the flames.

Suddenly the sound of a jet airplane came loudly
over the house! A terrifying sound they had never
ever heard before. Lucas felt as if a B52 was going
to land on the roof! Mr. Wilson yelled to the boys
as he jumped back from the fireplace. The chimney
was on fire! The flames were large and bright as
they climbed higher and higher up the cylinder!

"Everybody get outside," Mr. Wilson instructed
them calmly as he reached for the fire extinguisher.
The boys ran for their shoes and coats, as Mrs.

Wilson picked up little Mary Ellen, and made sure that no one else was inside their home. Mr. Wilson darted up the stairs, and pounded on each corner of the hallway window. Once it was loose, he stepped out cautiously onto the porch roof, and carefully climbed up onto the house roof with fire extinguisher in hand. The Orange and yellow inferno stretched up through the top of the chimney. They reached higher and higher as they fed off of the soot from inside! Mr. Wilson attacked it with no mercy. Spraying the foam from the extinguisher, he safely doused the blaze.

Mr. Wilson let out a sigh of relief as he gazed down upon his family waiting at the side of the house to see what would happen. Then he carefully trudged through the foot of snow on the rooftop and climbed back in through the window.

He met his family at the door and informed them that everything was safe now, and they could come back inside. The fire was out.

The boys couldn't help but notice that the snow had finally stopped falling. Mrs. Wilson had taken Mary Ellen to the Mall to see Santa Claus, so Brett approached his father, "Dad? If you're done settin' the house on fire, would you mind if we all went down to Curt's to snowmobile?"

Mr. Wilson was not amused. "Smart Asses don't get to do anything. They end up cleaning bathrooms and kitchens while their friends go without them."

Brett smiled at his dad. Mr. Wilson knew that Brett was only kidding, and that he was too young still to understand that there are certain times that sarcasm might not be appropriate.

"Please. I'm sorry dad."

Mr. Wilson looked over the freckled nose, and nodded. "But you all make sure you dress warm. And nobody rides without a helmet!" he yelled after them as they were already out the door.

The boys (Brett, Lucas and Jason) began their journey to Billson Drive while still dressing. Curt Ryan lived on the cal-de-sac at the other end of Hampton Mills. There was a large vacant lot behind his house that was perfect for snowmobiling. The boys trudged through the many feet of snow that had fallen on the town over the last five days. They climbed over giant snow banks yelling King of The Mountain, and then pushing each other off the top, but always mindful of the giant snow plows that pushed through town. Next they stopped along the way to create seats in the giant drifts as they imitated their fathers sitting in a bark-a-lounger with the 'clicker' in their hands, then laughed and moved on. They threw snowballs at each other, and then spent a few quiet moments just walking in the silence of the crisp winter wonderland.

By the time they reached Curt Ryan's house on Billson Drive, they were wet and exhausted, but that didn't matter. They had waited all summer for this snowfall. The first thing they did was fire up the snowmobile and then each took turns driving one full loop around the field followed by one good figure eight.

When Jason's older brother Joey showed up on his sled, they had the great idea of dog fighting. They found rope in Curt's garage and tied a plastic snow sled to the back of each snowmobile. Then, Joey driving his Ski-Doo with Jason on the sled, and Curt driving his machine with Brett on the back of that sled, they took off. Lucas stood watching as the two snowmobiles drove side by side, and the two sled riders fought to the death…or at least to knock the other one off. The fight was brutal, as they grabbed, pushed, kicked and pulled at each other, to become victorious. Finally Jason won!

They returned to the back yard, and let Lucas climb on board. He 'got winners,' so he was to take on Jason next. Again it was a fierce dog fight. Arms and legs flailed about as Jason finally pulled him off his sled. Jason was victorious again! He was the dog fight champ!

Lucas lay in the snow catching his breath. Finally he got to his feet covered in white flakey snow. Jason laughed hysterically holding his side. Lucas looked down at his clothes and started to laugh as well.

"It's the Stay Puff Marshmallow Man," Jason exclaimed pointing to the boy in white.

Lucas began bounding around the field with his heavy steps and stiff arms, as he impersonated the giant from Ghostbusters.

"Nobody steps on a church in my town!" Curt called out reliving the movie, and pretended to shoot Lucas with his laser gun.

"Come on you jackasses." The fun was interrupted when Joey waved them all back on to the sleds as he was in a hurry to return home.

They rounded the field once, before finding themselves back in Curt's yard, with Brett.

"Alright, ass cheese, I gotta get to work," Joey told his little brother and rode off on his snowmobile.

"Now what?" Lucas asked.

"Inner tube…." Curt said to Brett with a devilish grin.

Lucas looked over at Jason who was smiling the same way, and then to Brett, "what's that?" he asked.

"Oh nothing," Brett told him. "Just we tie the inner tube on and when you turn it glides way out…it's totally awesome," he said, the whole time pretending with his body to drive the snowmobile.

Curt ran through the deep snow to the shed and pulled out the large white inner tube, while Jason untied the plastic sled from the rope on the back of the remaining snowmobile. Curt took the end from Jason and tied it to the plastic handle on the side of the tube.

"Who's first?" Curt asked grinning.

Brett jumped on the snowmobile, "you go first Curt. You haven't gotten to ride yet."

Curt climbed aboard and held on tight. Brett put the black machine in motion and the doughnut shaped ride trailed swiftly behind. As they approached the first turn Brett had the foresight to start the turn early, so that the tube had enough room to swing out as it glided across the white field. Curt yelled out laughing the entire time.

Jason and Lucas stood waiting behind the house for them to return. Finally they came back for someone else to take their turn.

"Okay guys, let me drive Lucas around, and then we'll try one of us driving and three of us on the tube!" Jason suggested passionately.

They all agreed and Lucas took his seat on the inner tube. Jason straddled the seat of the snowmobile and pulled his face mask down. Before buckling his helmet onto his head, he quickly turned around in his black facemask that covered up over his nose and looked at the kid behind him. "Luuuuke…I am your Faaatthheerrr….," he said in his best Darth Vader voice. He giggled like a girl, with his prepubescent voice, and started the machine.

"Luke!" Curt yelled to him over the loud motor. "The powder on the top sucks. It was all blowin' up in my face. Turn your face mask around backwards!"

"Oh that'll be wild!" Brett yelled out.

Lucas Reed took the advice of a veteran inner tuber, and turned his yellow and black face mask around backwards. (He was not on the snowmobile, so a helmet was not 'required.')

Jason Sharper strapped on his helmet and pressed in the throttle. They were off! Once again, the white tube swept across the snow in the path from the snowmobile. Jason thought ahead the way that Brett had, and turned the sled early. The inner tube, swung way out, and just as Curt had done, Lucas yelled out into the frozen air and laughed wildly. As Jason approached North Street, his eye fixated on the high crest of the ditch alongside the road. He fiendishly grinned as his brow furrowed closer together. He had decided that he would get Lucas as close to the ditch as he thought he would be able to. The inner tube would fly up on the curve of the gully, and scare sightless Lucas…it was a playful joke; not maniacal. He drove into the turn and the tube started to drift out. Suddenly, Jason noticed a mailbox, atop a pole, planted *firmly* into the ground.

"Look out!" Jason shouted.

But Lucas was blind. With his mask on backwards he could see nothing. It was too late. The boy and the big white inner tube smacked into the mailbox! The young boy hit the pole spread eagle and took the blow to the groin. The inner tube was no match for the mailbox pole either. It popped and flew out in pieces scattered about the field.

Lucas lay in the road as Jason hit the break and killed the snowmobile engine. Brett and Curt let out a yell as they began running for North Street. Jason darted to Lucas' side, certain that he had killed him.

From out of the darkness, the small boy began to laugh. Ten year old Lucas Reed, came to and just began laughing uncontrollably as he pulled off his mask.

"What the hell was that," he asked.

Jason fell to his knees grabbing his stomach in relief. "Are you okay?"

Lucas lifted his head and saw the mailbox. "I think I'm gonna have a bruise."

Brett and Curt reached the other two boys and were relieved to find Lucas alive...and laughing none the less. They fell into the snow and the four lay there laughing.

"Luke man. I'm so sorry. I just thought it'd be funny to throw ya up on the side of the ditch. Cause you couldn't see anything." Jason took a breath, "I never thought about the mailboxes. Dude, I'm sorry."

Lucas continued to laugh, "that's okay,"

Jason sat upright in the snow, and looked at the inner tube scattered everywhere. "Dude, is your dad gonna be pissed?"

Curt shook his head. He didn't care.

Jason started laughing again as he picked up the only recognizable part left of the tube. He held up the black plastic handle and added, "I told you we shouldn't have crossed the streams." Another Ghostbusters reference, as he was pelted with snowballs.

"When were they coming?" Lucas asked

"They said they were on their way," Brett answered.

They played a game of H.O.R.S.E. while they waited for the Cooper brothers so that Lucas could work on his shooting skills. Small Mary Ellen Wilson was playing all alone with her baby doll on the swing set. The Wilson parents had gone out to dinner with Mr. and Mrs. Reeves leaving Tommy in charge. He of course, was in the house talking to some girl on the phone, but felt pretty secure that someone was watching his little sister. Brett was...sort of.

Finally Joe and Paul Cooper showed up on their bikes; fully equipped with the cards in their spokes making all kinds of racket. They quickly tossed their bicycles on the lawn and joined in the game. They zigged and zagged around the court, dribbling and passing continually, as each took random shots at the rim.

"Brett, can I go over to Christie's house?" the seven year old girl appeared in the middle of the basketball court.

"No."

"Why not?" she demanded.

"I don't know. Because." Brett looked at the house where Tommy sat peacefully inside. "I'm not watching you. Tommy is...go ask him."

Mary Ellen pouted as she stood in the middle of the court; her nappy blonde hair blowing in her face. Brett dribbled around her once, but then on his next turn brushed right past her, "Move," he yelled.

"No!" she yelled back. "I wanna play Brett," she whined.

"No. Now get lost. My friends are here."

Mary Ellen dropped her face pitifully and began to walk away. "Wait." She heard Joe call out to her. Turning with her saddened lower lip pushed out, she faced Joe Cooper.

Joe looked over at Brett, "What time is it?"

"I don't know."

"Well when we left it was about four," Paul answered.

Joe looked over at the Church and felt an imaginary light bulb click on above his head. "Mary Ellen we'll play with ya."

Brett's brow furrowed. As he started to object Joe cut him off with his hand raised towards him. Brett closed his mouth and waited. "Come on Mary Ellen," he put his arm around her tiny shoulder and walked her over to the side porch steps. Next Joe went into the garage and snooped around a bit before hitting the jackpot he was in search of. He reappeared from the garage with a devilish grin and told the group what game they would play.

"Okay Mary Ellen. We're the bad guys," he started. "Were gonna pretend like we're cowboys. Outlaws," he added with a big facial gesture. Mary Ellen smiled. "We'll rob the bank, and use you as a hostage. Do you know what that means?"

Mary Ellen nodded, "I'll be the damsel in distress," she said confidently.

"Yeah…." Joe smiled at her, charming her socks off. "Okay. Now you stand over by the window and pretend like you're at the bank getting money."

Mary Ellen went over to the porch window and made believe that she was conversing with the bank teller.

Joe gathered the boys to the back side of the house. "Paul, in the garage, next to Snoot's food, is a rope. Grab it," he instructed.

"Whose Snoot?" Lucas asked.

"My Dog."

"You have a dog?"

"Yeah," Brett nodded. Turning his attention to Joe, "What the hell are we doing?" he asked.

"Just play along. Trust me."

Paul returned with the rope, and Joe pointed his index finger out like a gun. "Okay outlaws. Let's take this bank," and he laughed wickedly as they stormed into 'the bank' to rob it. Joe and Paul pretended to hold the bank tellers at gun point as Brett and Lucas watched the doors and the captured patrons they had ordered to the floor. They laughed aloud as they took turns yelling and pretending to kick mouthy hostages. As they gathered the remaining money bags, the Sheriff appeared at the door!

"We've got you surrounded Clarey Gang," Lucas yelled pretending to be the sheriff from outside.

"You'll never take us alive sheriff," Joe responded calmly.

"Papa! There's four men with guns!" Mary Ellen yelled out.

"Papa, huh?" Joe looked triumphantly at the little girl that would become his hostage. He grabbed her (gently) by the arm and pretended to hold the gun to her side. "You're coming with us darlin'."

Paul took the game next, "Sheriff! We're coming out. And we got your girl hostage. So don't shoot," he instructed. The outlaw group made their way to the bank door and pushed their way through using little Mary Ellen Wilson (the sheriff's daughter) as a shield. Lucas was the last one out, holding his gun on the group inside the bank until they were all safely outside. Then Joe acted as though he was hoisting the young girl up onto his trusty steed and they all galloped off...up Clarey Ave.

As they neared the stop sign they halted their imaginary horses. "What are we gonna do with the

128

girl?" Lucas asked in his southern outlaw voice. "We can't take her with us. She'll slow us down." He looked around at the scoundrel group, "We can't send her back none neither. She knows what we look like."

"Luke's got a good point gang," Joe said. "Here's what we'll do." He stepped down from the pretend horse and helped the lady off as well. The rest of the men dismounted and followed. Joe led the damsel to the telephone pole in the middle of the rectory parking lot across Clarey Ave from the church. "Paulie. You got that rope on ya?" he asked.

Paul took the rope from his saddle horn and tossed it to his brother Joe.

"Okay Mary Ellen. Now you stand up against this pole and I'm gonna tie ya to it," he said as sweetly as he could.

"Nooo," Mary Ellen said timidly.

"It's okay El. The good guys are comin' and they're gonna save you." He stepped back from her and added, "Damsel in distress, right?"

Mary Ellen thought for a moment and then agreed against her better judgment. How could she be rescued by a white knight if she were never in distress (she may have had her girl meets boy fairytales mixed up a bit.) Mary Ellen stood against the pole and let Joe tie her securely in place.

"Okay kid. Now be tough," he said quietly to her, then stepped back.

"We'll leave her here like this. The Sun'll be beatin' down soon and she'll start to cook. Then the Vultures'll start prayin' on her," he yelled to the others. "That is if the Coyotes don't get her first." Then he turned to the others and whispered., "or the old ladies." He grinned and mounted his horse's back. Together they rode off, leaving her there stranded, tied to the telephone pole.

They rode back to the house and out of sight.

"So what now Joe?" Paul asked.

"Well maybe the good guys will come and rescue her."

The three other boys looked skeptically at the fourth.

"Or...," he started. "Maybe an old lady."

"An old Lady?" Lucas questioned.

Just then a car pulled into the parking lot. Joe pointed to the sign, "It's Bingo Night boys!"

The boys started roaring. Holding their stomachs with side splitting laughter they headed towards the house on the other side of the parking lot and hid behind the brush. Then they quietly crouched down and peered through the bushes as the little girl tied to the telephone pole began to cry.

Cars filed into the rectory parking lot one by one.
Each unloading seniors as they prepared for their
favorite night of the week. Each one walking past
the poor little soul strapped to the creosoted pole;
each one looking sideways at her, but doing nothing
to help. Mary Ellen's normally bright blue eyes
were red and tear soaked as she began to wale
heavily. The boys looked on as they tried to control
their laughter. Finally a pair of sweet older women
stopped to inquire about the girl. As the boys
watched them slowly work through the knots to
untie her they ran for home. They mounted their
bicycles and tore through the parking lot on the east
side of the church.

Mary Ellen ran home in tears.

"I got it, I got it!" Lucas yelled as he rode across the church parking lot.

In school that day, Jason had told Brett and Lucas a story he had heard, a sort of urban legend of the eighties to scare candy loving kids. Lucas was the only one with any money on him, so he was double dog dared to go to McCoy's Market and get supplies. Lucas had strict orders from his mother to never cross the bridge in town. That was as far as she wanted him to venture from home. But this was a double dog dare... and you can't back down from those...everyone knows that, even moms. He very timidly rode away from his friends across the lot. He looked both ways, not for cars, but for signs of his mother. Then he pulled out onto North Street, peddled as fast as he could to McCoy's and hid his bike on the side of the building. He purchased his goods and rode home like the wind.

Back at the church lot, he ditched his bike and ran to where Jason and Brett waited with Joe and Paulie Cooper on the back porch steps. Joe and Paul were late to hear this day's adventure, so they sat quietly waiting to see what was up. Lucas took off his backpack and pulled out the packet of Pop Rocks. Then he reached in again and pulled out two cans of TAB cola. Lucas grinned.

"No way," Paulie said with surprise. "You can't do that dude. Some kid died from that!"

"No they didn't," Joe said to him with disgust.

"Ya-huh," Jason said with his eyes wide and mouth open. "And not just some kid. Micky!"

"Micky! Who the hell is Micky?" Joe asked.

"You know," Brett nudged his arm, "the kid that eats all the cereal. Micky likes it," he repeated the catch phrase from the commercials.

"He died? From Pop Rocks and Cola?" Joe asked skeptically.

They all nodded in unison, then stared down at the bag of rocks.

Jason looked at Lucas, "Okay, who's first?"

"Not me man. I got the crap. Someone else is doin' this."

"Paulie'll do it," Joe declared.

Paul Cooper shook his little blonde head.

"We all do it," Brett said with certainty. "We'll open the Rocks, each poor some in our hands, and then pass the TAB around."

They each looked timidly at one another, and then agreed. To make it ceremonious, they walked out to the center of the back yard and formed a circle. They sat Indian Style with the TAB and the Pop Rocks in the center. Then one at a time, they passed the bag of rocks around the circle, and poured equal amounts out into their hands. They compared them several times, to make sure no one was 'wussing out.'

"Now," Jason told them. "We put the rocks on our tongues and swallow them down. Then we chug the soda."

"Count of three," Brett said. "One. Two...Three."

They each tipped their heads back and placed the Pop Rocks on their tongues. Being young boys though, they were completely unable to swallow them down without first listening to the fizzle in their mouths. Next, Lucas popped open the TAB, took down a giant gulp, and passed it to Jason. Both sodas continued around the circle until they were gone, then the kids laid back on the green carpet of grass and waited for imminent death. And waited. And waited. Nothing happened.

Joe Cooper sat back up and looked at the others still lying in the face of death.

"Anybody's stomach explode yet?" Jason asked.

They all sat up in disappointment, as the blue bomber pulled into the driveway. Tommy and Dave stepped out of the car, as Robbie darted out the side door to greet them. They stood huddled together for a moment before moving inside. As they passed by the boys, they noticed them sitting in a circle, pausing briefly in wonderment before carrying on. "They'll never let us go," they overheard Tommy say. Next they saw Dave shrug his shoulders and reply, "Then we'll sneak out."

Lucas whipped his head around to Brett as they both recalled the night last fall when they caught them stealing the car. The older Wilson brothers had gone into the house.

Jason, while disappointed that no one exploded, decided that the project was not a total loss. They still had one small packet of Pop Rocks left. He poured them into each one of their hands, and they tossed them in their mouths. They sat in their circle with their jaws open as they fizzled and popped on their tongues. When Tommy, Dave and Robbie all reappeared in the back yard, they yelled to the group of kids. They each turned around to face the brothers with their mouths open and the fizz drooling down their chins like rabid beasts. Rolling their eyes, the teenagers walked away.

It was decided earlier in the day that Lucas would spend the night again with Brett, and they would go early Saturday morning with Mrs. Wilson to the mall to play in the arcade while she shopped. They played pool downstairs for a while but decided to go hang out in Brett's room upstairs before hitting the sack. They popped in the newest Foreigner cassette tape and settled in. Lucas had grabbed Robbie's Rubik's cube off his dresser and messed with that, as Brett tried to get his newest Transformer to change into a warrior.

Brett's older brothers systematically filed through the room in age order. Tommy barreled through and opened the window. Robbie behind him grabbed his jacket from his bed, as Dave, who was last to enter the room, climbed through the window first. Lucas sat motionless on the floor with the cube. Brett laid back on the bed with his toy and continued to mess with it, as they piled out of the second story window, looking up only once. When they had all finally passed through, Brett got off the bed without a word, and closed the window behind them.

Lucas looked up at him confused, "what's ... goin' on?" he asked hesitantly.

"Oh," Brett laughed. "My brothers are going somewhere." He sat back on the bed with his warrior. "See they climb down the tree, and I leave the window open just that tiny bit so they can get back in when they come home...and *we* know how they get to where they're going," he added with a great big smile and raised red eyebrows.

Lucas smiled and laughed at the genius. There it was again. These brothers had this whole place wired. They knew every trick, and seemed to always have each other's backs. *How cool,* Lucas thought.

The boys eventually found themselves under their covers listening to the radio as they drifted off to sleep. Brett listened as his Dad was up and moving about the house. Then he heard a strange noise from outside the house. Earlier Brett found himself feeling sleepy. His brothers were not home yet, so he opened the window for them before he climbed into bed. Now, with the sound of something outside, he leapt to his feet and over to the window. He looked down to see Dave getting back to his feet at the base of the tree where he had fallen. "Dad's up," he tried to call down to them in a loud whisper, but the teenagers heard nothing from the second story. Suddenly Brett felt a hand on his shoulder; a large hand! He turned around in fear as he saw his father standing over him.

"On the bed," was all that he said as he pointed in the darkness.

Brett ran over and sat next to Lucas who had already climbed up off the floor and sat nervously. Mr. Wilson moved to the doorway and stood silently in the dark. He waited as the first figure climbed through the opening (Tommy). Then he still did not move as the next one stepped over the ledge and onto the carpeting (Robbie). As the last kid reached over the window sill with his upper body, Tommy turned to help him...the lights flipped on. All three boys froze. Tommy with one hand on Dave; Dave half in the window, and Robbie removing his sneakers! They looked up slowly at the six foot five man in the doorway. Mr. Wilson said nothing. He turned off the light, and left the room. He went into his bedroom, put on his clothes, and headed downstairs.

Tommy finished helping Dave in through the window, as all three boys remained in the spot where they entered. They were afraid to leave the room, and the two younger boys were afraid to move at all. They listened as Mr. Wilson went downstairs and then heard the screen door slam behind him.

"What's he doing?" Robbie asked quietly.

Tommy and Dave just shrugged their shoulders.
Mrs. Wilson came down the hall in her robe. She
stopped at the doorway and turned on the light
switch. She found her three older sons standing
fully dressed by the window, and the two younger
boys scared on the bed. "What did you do?" she
asked with disgust, then turned the light back off
and ran downstairs after her husband.

Not long after she stormed away, they heard the
attempt of a motor. "What was that?" Tommy
asked aloud.

"It sounded like a dirt bike," Robbie answered with
confusion.

They heard it again.

"That's a chainsaw!!" Brett cried out as he flew off
his bed and pushed through his brothers towards the
window. They all stood around the window staring
through the cool pane of glass as Mr. Wilson started
the chainsaw at three a.m. that morning, and
disassembled their escape route.

He worked on the tree until four in the morning,
when a town cop, finally came by and demanded
that he stop…neighbors had called in, complaining
about the noise.

Get A Grip

The fifth grade class gathered in the hallway as they awaited the first bell. The girls shifted about together with their usual nonsense and giggling as the boys gathered around listening to the story of the great escape tree being cut down in the middle of the night. Beverly Moore pushed her way into the group of young men to announce their latest social activity. The girls had decided to reenact the previous summer's Hands Across America (which never went through J.D.W.). The boys rolled their eyes and told her to get lost…there was no way they were doing something so stupid.

Then Neil Norton had an idea.

He gathered the boys close and very carefully explained his plan. They loved it! He tucked his white shirt into his black jeans, and with confidence he strutted out of the group in his cowboy boots and headed into enemy territory while 'his boys' watched on.

"Hey Bev," he called out to her.

She turned to him with anger still on her face from the previous rejection.

Neil looked back at the guys and told her with great compassion and understanding, "Hey Bev. We're sorry about that before. It actually sounds cool, and you can count us in."

Beverly's face brightened at the news as the other girls gathered around closer to listen.

"Okay," she started with excitement. "So we'll do this today at recess. Between us, the sixth grade and the fourth grade, we want to see how far we'll stretch."

"Oh. You mean it's not just us?" he asked.

"No. What would be the purpose in that?"

Neil didn't see any purpose in any of it, but he played along. They would do this at recess that afternoon.

Neil Norton returned to his gang and told them of this new development. They decided to keep their plan only to themselves, as they didn't think the fourth graders could be trusted, and the sixth graders might actually *want* to do this thing.

School carried on as normal, with only the small interruptions of chatter about the big event. During lunch, Lucas found himself standing behind Jana Harris in the milk line. He leaned in over her shoulder and whispered something quietly into her ear. Jana turned and looked at him but asked no questions. She carried on with her purchase and found her normal seat at the table with her friends. As she sat eating her lunch, she looked over to Lucas several times. Each time she caught his eyes, he smiled and looked away.

The time in the cafeteria came and went very quickly and before long everyone found themselves on the playground gathering in their different grades…of course boys in one cluster, girls in another. Mr. Hill's secretary had come out with her camera to capture the big event on film forever.

They decided to stretch the line across the playground behind the equipment. As they ventured out behind the swings, Carrie Warbelle and Michelle Remarc skipped by holding hands yelling to everyone that it would look best if they were to line up boy, girl, boy, girl.

That was what the boys were counting on.

With the fourth graders on one end, and the upper classmen sixth graders on the other, the lady fifth graders formed a line in between and waited for the shy group of young men that gathered one last time before taking their positions.

They walked with great enthusiasm up to the line and they each took their spots in between the girls, letting their hands hang loosely at their sides.

Before taking his spot, Lucas found Jana one last time with his dark eyes, and shook his head very subtly. She stood in her blue jean overalls with her hands folded neatly in front of her and wondered what they were up to, but kept it all to herself.

The fourth grade teacher, Mrs. Kenzington, stood in front of the long line and gave the word for them to join hands. The boys were perfect. They reached out...then they stopped. Looking down the line at one another, every single fifth grade boy reached up with both his hands and cupped them over their mouths. Then in one quick action they reached down and grabbed on to their hands to hold.

The girls stood with their feet together and gigantic smiles. Gigantic smiles that very quickly dropped from their faces, as Christina Stampard was the first to cry out in disgust! One by one each girl screamed into the warm spring air. Each young girl darted from the perfect line as they ran wiping wads of spit from their palms on to their pants and skirts. Some even burst into tears!

Mr. Hill's Secretary caught it all on film.

The boys laughed hysterically, some actually falling to the ground with splitting sides. The fourth graders caught wind of the 'spit grip' and started roaring as well. The sixth graders found themselves divided. Some too found it hysterical, while some were angered at the immaturity, while still others were only angered that they didn't think of it first.

As the girls ran flailing about, Lucas sat on the green grass wiping the laughter tears from his eyes. He noticed only one girl was not panicked. His girl. Jana stood in the same spot with her hands still neatly folded in front of her, as she laughed at the sight.

Recess was over.

Every Action 15

The plan for the day was to hang out at the Cooper's house. Lucas very carefully explained to his mother that they lived beyond the bridge, and that he and Brett would be riding there together, if she would please allow it.

Not completely comfortable with her ten year old riding to a location she wasn't familiar with, she instead offered to bring the boys over to Joe and Paul's house to play that afternoon. Mrs. Reed dropped them both off and told them she would be back around supper time to pick them up.

Once out of the car and through the boyish, 'what's up' greetings, the young men decided to warm up for a day of hard core play and mischief, with their usual game of hoops. Lucas was greatly improving. His free throws were much more accurate, and he was quickly mastering *the pass without looking move,* that Brett had tried to teach him.

Mr. Cooper had the week off from work and was busy cleaning out their house for Mrs. Cooper's garage sale the following weekend. Occasionally he would call on them to help carry things out to the garage. As Paul, Brett and Lucas passed the orange ball, Joe carried an old TV cart up from the basement and set it in the garage. He checked it out from every angle, and then took both hands and pushed hard against the top of it checking it for stability.

"Hey guys," he called to the others. Waving them over he added, "check this thing out."

"What is it?" Lucas asked.

"It's the cart the TV used to sit on downstairs," Paul told them.

"So what about it, Joe?" Brett chimed in.

Joe wheeled it out onto the lawn and jumped up on top of it. "See," he said with a large grin.

The other three boys looked at him with raised eyebrows in confusion. Joe pointed down the hill in front of them and then grabbed on tight to either side, "give me a push."

The boys quickly figured out what he had in mind. Lucas moved around to the other side, while Brett moved to the back and Paul took hold of the side where he was standing. They counted to three and then pushed as hard as they could. Joe Cooper let out a yell as he went flying down the small hill that was their side yard. The other three boys ran behind him, as the cart finally fell over at the bottom of the hill and Joe tumbled off laughing.

"Cool!" Paul cried out, "My turn!"

They pushed the old TV cart back up the hill and this time Paul climbed on board. He too grabbed on tightly as the other three pushed his little figure down the hill. This time the cart didn't go quite as far before tipping over. Rushing back to the top, Brett jumped on top. Brett being the heaviest, Joe got behind him with Lucas and Paul on either side, and they pushed as hard as they could.

The cart wheeled down wildly almost tipping over twice. As it barreled down, Brett clung tightly to the sides. Suddenly he heard a snap...then a pop...then the cart plummeted down, collapsing upon itself. As the cart collapsed, Brett shouted out as his right hand was pinched in the metal frame.

The other boys came running after him in a panic. Brett lay in the green grass with his hand stuck in the cart while withering in pain. As they reached him, Joe and Lucas fell to their knees, as they looked closely at the blood and decided to try and free their friend's hand. Paul ran for a grown up.

Lucas and Joe carefully pulled the fallen TV cart apart as Brett slid his hand out from its entrapment. Joe froze at the sight, as Lucas had the opposite reaction and started to yell! The tip of his finger was gone! Brett took one look at his hand that was bleeding and causing him so much pain, and he yelled out again even louder!

Mr. and Mrs. Cooper came quickly and wrapped his hand in a towel. Mrs. Cooper got Brett carefully to the car, as the boys' father gently picked up the finger tip that was lying still inside the folded cart.

Joe and Paul climbed in the front seat beside their father as their mother held Brett in the back seat keeping pressure on his hand. Ghostly white Lucas climbed in carefully next to him as his stomach churned. They sped through Hampton Mills back to Clarey Ave, where Lucas darted from the car and ran as fast as he could to the house to get Brett's parents.

"Mr. Wilson…Mrs. Wilson…Come Quick!" he yelled to them.

Mr. Wilson was still at work, but Brett's mother ran to the door quickly to see what the small boy was yelling about. Mrs. Cooper had carefully helped the red haired boy from the car and was waiting by the station wagon. Mr. Cooper stood there as well, armed with the finger tip.

"I don't know what happened Mary," Mrs. Cooper started to explain.

Mrs. Wilson ran to her son, but he would not let her take the wrap off his hand. His normal white freckled face was paler then it had ever been.

"They were playing on this old cart thing we have and next thing I know…" she stopped to look at Brett's white face. "Mary, he cut the tip of his finger off."

Mrs. Wilson gasped, as Mr. Cooper held up a towel with the finger inside. She panicked only for a split second before ordering everyone into the car. Once again Mrs. Cooper climbed into the back seat with Brett and Lucas, while Joe and Paul, again, sat up front. Mrs. Wilson started the station wagon, as Mr. Cooper reached through the window and started to pass the finger tip through to his oldest son Joe. Then he hesitated and pulled his arm back handing it to Paul.

"Do not play with it," he ordered him with great authority.

148

She backed the car out of the drive way and headed up Clarey Ave towards the stop sign. Lucas watched out the window as that same menacing, mangy brown dog sat in the Parish Hall parking lot. He felt the eyes of the mutt stare down on him as the car rolled slowly past.

As they reached the Emergency room, Mrs. Cooper and Mrs. Wilson ushered the young boy inside and found him a seat. Mrs. Wilson went right to the window check in as Mrs. Cooper waited with Brett and the other boys…only having to remind them once, not to play with the finger.

The thought of the severed finger made Lucas sick. Every time he thought of Paulie sitting there holding somebody's finger…even if it were just the tip… made him feel like he would vomit. *Be cool,* he kept telling himself. *Puking now would not be a cool thing to do. Although you are in a hospital…*

Finally Brett was called in and the kind nurse took the wrapped up finger tip from little Paul Cooper.

"Every action…" Lucas overheard Mrs. Cooper say shaking her head with a sigh as she settled into the waiting room chair.

He pondered what she had said. Then he thought back to Garfield, and his poster in Mr. Rockwell's classroom. Finally he asked. "Ma'am, what did you just say?"

"Oh nothing Lucas."

It wasn't nothing, and he needed someone to explain Garfield's wisdom to him once and for all. "Mrs. Cooper, you said, 'Every action'. What did you mean by that?"

The small framed woman looked down at him and took in a deep breath. "Every action," she started and then paused again, "has an equal reaction. Or something like that."

"Every action has an equal and opposite reaction," he corrected her.

"Yes," she nodded.

"What does that mean?"

"I'm sorry?"

"What does that mean? Every action has an equal and opposite reaction…what does that mean?" he asked again.

"Oh." Mrs. Cooper leaned back and thought how to explain Newton's famous law. She brushed her platinum hair behind her ear and gave it a shot. "Well. It means exactly what it says. For every action you take…like riding on a TV cart down a hill for example. There is an equal and opposite reaction…like getting your finger lopped off."

Lucas pulled his head back into his neck like a turtle as he thought about the logic, but still did not quite get it. Mrs. Cooper could see the lack of clarity in his young face. "It's like saying that everything you do will bring on something else. Like everything in life is a chain reaction. I guess it's a way of saying look before you leap. Because whatever you do will trigger something else, and it may not always be pleasant."

Lucas nodded along as it made some sense finally to him, then added, "Like loosing your finger."

"Don't say that. My God. That's a terrible thing to say. I'm sure they can put it back on somehow."

Lucas sat back and stared at all the posters on all of the walls of the emergency room waiting area. Finally he understood Garfield. Then he figured he better ask while he had the captive audience.

"Can I ask you something else?"

"Sure honey. What's up?" she said with a smile.

"Ignorance is bliss. What's that mean?"

She furrowed her brow, "Ignorance is bl…Oh…you mean, ignorance is NOT bliss," she corrected him. That one she pondered for a moment before answering. "Well. Take it apart. What does Ignorance mean?"

Lucas shrugged his shoulders, as he had no idea.

"Well, ignorance means, that you don't have knowledge of something. Like…" she searched for an example. "Ok. Like I don't know how to fix a car. So I am ignorant when it comes to auto repair. Okay? "

Lucas nodded again.

"And bliss means happy," she looked at the small dark eyes to see if he was piecing any of it together. He was obviously still at a loss. "Ignorance, not knowing about something, is not bliss. So if you don't know about something, that doesn't exactly mean that you're happy. It just means that you don't know any different. You understand?"

Lucas shook his head.

"Where are you getting these things kid?" she asked.

"They're posters on the wall in my classroom."

"Ohhh…" she sat back with a bit more enlightenment. "I think what they are trying to tell you there, is that knowledge is power, and not knowing will make you less happy then if you do know…you know?" she laughed.

Lucas began to nod along. She was starting to make some sense. But at least Garfield was clearer.

"I'll have to talk to your teachers. They really need to explain those posters if they're gonna hang them up." She smiled kindly at the young man as Mrs. Wilson reappeared with Brett and all ten fingers. They had stitched the tip back on…it would just always be a little crooked.

Do You Smell That?　　　16

Lucas Reed lay in bed that night and starred at his ten fingers by the light of the moon. He folded different ones down imaging what it would be like to loose one. Suddenly the lull in the darkness was broken by the ringing of the telephone. Lucas glanced at his clock…it was 11:33. He took short, shallow breaths and tried to hold them as long as he could, trying desperately to hear the muffled sound through the walls. Finally he realized that it was his father calling. Anxious to tell his dad about the excitement of his day, he darted from his Star Wars bed sheets and ran to his mother's side.

His father had only a few minutes to talk before his plane left, so Lucas was unable to share his story, but he was on his way home from Europe and he would see him that next day!

Lucas could barely sleep. He no longer thought about his ten digits, but instead about his father. He had not seen him in months, and in a matter of hours, they were going to be a family again. He woke before his alarm clock sounded, ate his Lucky Charms, dressed quickly in his nicest cloths, and waited on the couch.

His mother, he felt, was taking forever as he watched the hands on the Grandfather clock click slowly by. Finally, she told him to go outside and find something to do. His father's flight would not be in for three more hours. With a heavy sigh, Lucas walked out onto the front porch and sat with his head heavy in his hands. *Three hours to kill…man that sucks*, he thought to himself. He walked up and down the short driveway and kicked at some stones...then he looked at his bike resting up against the garage. *I'll just be careful to stay clean*, he said to himself. He hopped on his bike and peddled his way through the Manor, up English Road, and stopped at the sign. He looked both ways and then pressed on to Clarey Ave.

As he casually peddled Lucas heard the sound of laughter and kids yelling behind him. He glanced under his arm, to see the bowling alley bullies, Jim Woodcock and his sidekick Porker riding up on him fast. Too Fast! Lucas laid down into the handle bars and pushed hard. *I just need to make it to Clarey Ave...they won't dare touch me there*, he thought. As they neared the small boy, big, stupid Porker, reached over with a small stick and stuck it through the spokes of Lucas' bike wheel. The wheel locked up and Lucas flew over the handle bars as the bike crashed over top of him!

He lay there for a moment as he felt the pavement rash burning on his face and hands, and wondered if he had broken anything. The two hoodlums, jumped from their bikes, throwing them onto the nearby lawn as Lucas rolled over slowly, grimacing in pain. As he opened his eyes, Woodcock and Porker were standing over him. This was the end...Lucas could feel it.

As Jim Woodcock fell to his knees he grabbed Lucas by his dress shirt collar and pulled him up off the ground so they could be face to face. "Well, don't you look sweet today," he teased. "All dressed up are ya?"

Lucas looked him cold in the eyes. He knew he didn't have a fighting chance, but the last thing he would do would be back down, or even worse, beg for mercy. His face and hands were burning, and he was fairly certain that there was blood seeping through his trousers from his left knee. Woodcock pulled back his right fist, as Lucas prepared for the first blow. Still looking him dead in the eye, he noticed something suddenly change. The beast of a boy had frozen and was no longer looking down into his face with hatred. Instead his eyes had grown wide and scared. He took a few gasping breaths before dropping Lucas back to the pavement and running for his bike. Woodcock never took his eyes off whatever had caught his attention. He never turned his back. He backed up quickly to his ride, and the two took off like their pants were on fire.

Lucas had no idea what had happened. He only knew the pain his young body was in. He rolled over from his right side onto his back, and gazed only for a second at the clear blue sky. Then he heard a noise…he turned his head to find that mangy brown dog only a few feet away. The dog was crouched in a defensive, attack position and his eyes were locked on the figures that were fading farther and farther away. His mouth slightly open, Lucas could smell his breath…what he was certain was the flesh of young boys. He scrambled to his feet, and grabbed his bicycle. He climbed aboard only to find the wheel wouldn't turn. He reached down without taking his eyes off the mutt and removed the stick from his spokes and rode away fast.

As Lucas approached the turn leading back down English Road, he realized that it was the dog that saved him. The dog had scared Woodcock and Porker away, and saved his life. He stopped short of the turn, and placed his foot to the ground. Lucas turned back and looked at the dog, who had relaxed his large body and was sitting quietly on the side of the road. He never advanced on Lucas. He never threatened him. Instead he lowered his head, stood back up, and strolled away.

He felt bad that he had run. The beast was protecting him, although why, he did not know, and all he did was run scared, instead of thanking him. But the mutt was gone. Afraid to go home looking like he did, he turned through Jason's yard and rode across the lawn, behind the Parish Hall and into the Wilson's driveway, where Robbie and Dave were standing.

"Hey, come to check out the finger?" Robbie joked.

Lucas tossed his bike to the ground instead of respectfully standing it up, out of the way like he usually did. He barreled past the teenagers and threw himself down heavily on the steps.

"What the hell happened to you?" Dave asked.

Lucas shook his head, never looking up. He felt as if he were going to cry, but would not allow it.

"Hey!" Robbie said to him again, demanding a response. "Luke what happened to ya?"

Dave opened the door and yelled into Brett to come outside. He came through the door, with Mary Ellen on his heels and Tommy followed right behind him.

"Holy crap, man what happened to ya?" Tommy asked.

"Nothing," he replied.

"It doesn't look like nothing," Mary Ellen answered him.

"I fell off my bike Mary Ellen, okay?" he told them. "Now go back inside."

"It doesn't look like you just fell off your bike," she responded in her tiny little voice.

"Well." He shook his head, and pulled at his shirt, "I did. This is what falling off your bike looks like," he continued with much more anger as he left his perch and walked away.

"Mary Ellen, go back inside please," Dave requested.

The little girl crossed her arms indignantly and stormed away in a huff.

Brett walked over to his friend and asked him one more time what had happened. Lucas gently touched his face in an effort to wipe it clean, but to no avail. Taking a deep breath he lifted his chin and looked at each one of the Wilson brothers gathered around him with concern. He sniffed once, and twitched his nose, then began, "Woodcock and Porker shoved me off my bike. They were gonna have at me, but then this dog scared em away."

The brothers looked at each other as if they understood exactly what went down.

"Why are you all dressed up?" Brett asked the small boy.

"My dad's coming home today."

That was it. That was more then enough information. They looked once again at each other in a way that meant they recognized what had happened and at the same time clarified what needed to happen next.

"Brettie, take Lucas in the house and get him cleaned up," Robbie instructed.

Then the three eldest Wilson's climbed in the blue bomber of a car and drove away.

"Where are they going?" he asked his friend.

Brett watched the car drive away, before adding, "They'll take care of this." Then he led his friend in the house and took him to his mother to ask her to help get him cleaned up to greet his father…of course only mentioning that he fell from his bike, and not ever telling her how he met the pavement.

The boys from Clarey Ave drove around Hampton Mills, combing every street, alley and long hidden driveway. Finally they found Porker by the railroad tracks off a dead end road….relieving himself.

As they filed out of the blue car, Porker noticed them from the corner of his eye. He nervously finished his business and shouted into the woods for his friend. The three boys met up with the fat kid, as Robbie emerged from the pack and met him face to face, while the other two hung back. "Where's your tough little friend?" he asked.

Suddenly stumbling out of the woods, laughing something about a chipmunk, Jim Woodcock came from the woods and froze in his tracks at the sight of the three large brothers. Dave walked over to him and stood toe to toe.

Tommy began to stroll casually around them as he began what would be today's lesson, "So you think it's fun to pick on little kids, huh?" he asked at first. "You think it's funny to push them off their bikes? How'd it be if we started pushing you around?"

Porker, stood nervously, as he uttered his case, "I didn't touch the kid," he begged to Robbie.

"Did you push him off his bike, or did he?" Robbie asked him walking aggressively towards him. Porker backed up in fear. With raised eyebrows, he asked him again, "Well?" Porker looked to the ground, and he felt himself shaking.

The entire time, Woodcock stood solid up against Dave. He was too stupid to be scared. He was a bit crazy and would take on anyone, no matter their size. Finally he spoke out getting everyone's attention back on him, "Yeah. He pushed the little looser off his bike. But I was the one that was gonna knock the crap outa him…till that stupid dog showed up!" he yelled out.

Dave grabbed him by the collar of his shirt, the way that he had done to Lucas. "Wha'd you say about that dog?" he asked.

Tommy reached out and grabbed Dave's arm as if to tell him to back down. Then he grabbed the kid by his nasty, dark hair, and dragged him over towards his buddy throwing him to the dirt at Porker's feet. Bending over in his face, Tommy threatened them both one last time.

"You didn't touch him this time because of the dog. But what you need to understand, is that you will *never* touch him." He informed them with great power.

No one to this day ever speaks of what happened out there by the tracks. Woodcock and Porker were seen around town after that day, so it was apparent that they did not kill them, but what actually transpired has never been told. All that anyone does know, is that every time they see Jim Woodcock, one brother will ask the other if they smell something and the other brother will respond, *yes, it smells kinda like Piss*. Oh, and the Wilson brothers had two new bikes in the garage from that day forward.

160

Movin' On

Lucas returned home, cutting through behind the
Parish Hall and staying off the roads. His mother
greeted him with concern, and helped him get
changed into new cloths. Then they drove out to
the Air Base to meet his father. After a long and
tearful reunion, the happy threesome ventured
home. His dad told them all about Europe and gave
them presents he had picked up along the way, and
Lucas went on and on about everything that had
happened while he was gone…the chimney fire, the
inner tube, the hands across America thing in
school, and of course the finger. Finally exhausted,
he crawled into bed.

The next morning they sat together as Mom served
a large home style family breakfast. Mr. Reed
began to explain what was going to happen next to
their family. He reminded Lucas how they had
never intended to stay in Hampton Mills very long.
That he was told when they moved there, that it was
only for a short time…then came the big news. The
news that Lucas had forgotten was eventually going
to come. He was so happy in this place that he let
himself forget what it means to be in the military.
He had found a place he liked calling home, and he
had made himself the best friends he was certain he
would ever have. But his father finally said it. The
words fell from Mr. Reed's lips and Lucas just
could not stop them…they were moving.

Lucas protested strongly, "Why?" he asked. "Why
do we have to leave? Can't you talk to your boss?"
He took a breath. "Maybe just you can go, and
mom and I can stay here," he reasoned.

"Lucas," his mother said with great disapproval.

"Lucas Gerard, we're a family. I know this is hard, but we don't have a choice. We go where the government tells us son," his father told him. He took a deep calming breath, and then tried approaching the situation again, "Now I know this is hard on you. You and your Mom. But this is the way things are. You'll understand when you are older. Please just respect that this is what we have to do and make the most of the time you have left here with your friends."

Lucas stood up from the table very calmly, very methodically. He carried his plate over to the garbage, scrapped off his food, and placed it in the sink. Then he grabbed his baseball cap and walked out the door. He stayed away from his bicycle this time, and just walked down the middle of the road. As he neared the turn onto English Road, he felt his gate start to change. Suddenly he felt himself in a jog, then a run, finally in a full out gallop as he ran across the lawn behind the Parish Hall, past the baseball field and finally out into the woods to the secret fort. Once safely tucked into the woods, he sat in a bed of leaves, folded his knees up to his chest and cried.

Lucas spoke not a word of his big move to anyone. He never told Brett or Jason that he was leaving town. He simply continued upon his merry way, and when future plans for summer vacation were being made, he simply avoided the commitment.

Finally the last day of school had arrived. They emptied out their desks and lockers and walked one last time as fifth graders as the herd of sheep moved down the long hallway, past the supply closet, and out to their buses.

As they reached the circle where the buses were parked, Lucas ran out of line and fought his way through the unruly group of eager children. He grabbed Jana Harris by the hand. His heart stopped, *what am I doing?* He thought. He had planned this for days in his mind, but couldn't believe he was actually executing.

Jana looked into his deep brown eyes, as he fumbled for the words. "I just wanted to say," he started and then swallowed hard. "I'm glad...I'm glad I knew you. Thanks," and he smiled at her.

Jana returned the smile and just as she opened her mouth to ask why, Lucas quickly added, "Have a nice summer," and darted for his bus.

He walked down the aisle and found a seat with one kid in it...the freckled faced, second grader, repeater. *Oh hell no,* he thought to himself and continued on to the back of the bus where he found a seat with Brett. The kids were wild. Tearing up their notebooks and throwing them wildly around the school bus. Singing about *no more home work, no more books, no more teachers dirty looks...* They had a wild ride home, and for a short time, Lucas had forgotten about his plight.
Of course you can't escape the inevitable. Lucas arrived home to find his mom packing their things. The movers would be coming the next day to pack

the whole house, but she was sorting and packing things for the family to take with them in the car. The sight of it made Lucas sick. He changed quickly and made his way over to Clarey Ave.

He parked his bike and ran up the side porch steps where he ran into Mr. Wilson. He pointed to the basketball court out back where they could clearly see Brett dribbling away. Lucas took a deep breath and went out back to join his friend. They played one on one and Lucas held his own against the Larry Bird wanna be. Next Lucas suggested that they go for a bike ride. The two boys rode through town and out to the bridge where they had been fishing when Robbie rescued the baby deer. Lucas was quiet, and still said nothing to his friend.

Finally they returned to Clarey Ave, where they were called inside to have pizza. The whole Wilson family was there. Lucas thought how odd it was that they were all gathered in one room at the same time. An event he was certain happened quite often, but they were all so busy all the time, it was rare that they all be in one place at one time…and he was with them…he felt like an honorary member of the family and secretly wished it could always be that way.

After dinner Lucas and Brett rode their bikes over to Jason Sharper's house where the boys sat on the steps in the garage. He finally felt it was time to admit what was coming. Lucas finally told his two closest friends, "so Monday we're moving."

"Moving?" Jason asked. "Moving where?"

"Nebraska."

"What!?" he exclaimed.

Brett sat motionless.

"Yup. We're being relocated." Lucas tried to act like it was no big deal, "new adventure boys."

Brett squinted his eyes as the setting sun glared in through the open garage door, and glared up at his friend. "So just like that you're gone?"

Lucas pursed his lips tightly and nodded rhythmically.

"Monday? That's fast," he added. "They don't give ya much time do they."

"They give you enough time to empty the gas from the lawn mower and find a moving company," Lucas explained, choosing not to tell them that he had known for a few weeks.

"Wow." Was all Jason could say.

Brett seconded that wow, and Lucas repeated it a third time.

"Well we gotta make the most of this weekend then dude," Jason decided. "We gotta party!"

Lucas smiled, as Brett agreed with him.

They spent what was left of Friday and all of Saturday doing everything they could think of. They went fishing early Saturday morning. They played basketball, and got friends together for chase over behind the Parish Hall. They snuck out to the woods and gambled away all the acorns they could find on black jack. They had a 4 hour ping pong tournament in the garage. They did it all! They played everything they could think of, they sat and talked about all the stuff they could remember doing, and then Saturday night they curled up on the floor of the Wilson house, and watched Ghost Busters…again.

Sunday was much different though. For starters, Lucas needed to be home for a great deal of the day to help complete the packing of all of his worldly processions. Then when the boys all did get together they were too depressed to make it any fun. They went to the trestle bridge for a while and just sat with their feet dangling over the side.
Finally it was time to go home. Lucas promised to be by in the morning before they left to say good bye, and he walked home sorrowfully.

That night, as Lucas threw out his paper plate, because all the kitchen ware had been packed, the phone rang. It was Brett.

"I'm gonna need you to come over here tonight. And wear old cloths," he told Lucas.

Lucas got quiet and went into the other room as far as the cord would allow, "I can't man. They're never gonna let me go anywhere tonight. We're leaving in the morning."

"I didn't tell you to ask anyone…just be here."

Lucas heard a click and Brett was gone.

Lucas sat nervously all evening until it was time for bed. The more he thought about it, the more panic stricken he became. *Be Cool*, he kept saying to himself, *have you learned nothing here?* What was Brett up to? He went to bed early, pretending to be too upset with the situation to be around his parents any longer. Then he waited for just the right moment and he climbed out his window. He very carefully climbed over the ledge, and slid down the shingled siding which burned his belly a bit as he slid down. Then he quietly moved through his backyard, snuck through the other yards on the Manor until he felt it was safe for him to run right down the center of the road, and across the grass to Clarey Ave.

As he rounded the Parish Hall, he found Brett, his brothers, Jason, and both Cooper boys waiting for him on the screen porch. They grinned when the small boy came to the door and greeted him with excitement.

"What's going on?" Lucas asked curiously.

"We're glad you made it buddy," was all Brett said as he handed him a knit cap. "Put this on. You're on my team."

Lucas looked at the wadded up cap in his hand and had a flash back to the first day he met Brett Wilson in the hallway and he handed him his gym shorts.

He placed the cap on over his brown locks, and followed the masses out to the Parish Hall parking lot, as he saw Tommy tossing a football in the air.

Lucas' eyes grew wide, as they each took their place on the line of scrimmage, and Midnight Football commenced. They played for hours. Laughing, tackling each other, scoring, piling on top of each other for scores, tackles, fumbles, sometimes just for the sake of piling on top of each other. At one point Lucas lay there in the parking lot looking up at the summer night sky, and just grinned from ear to ear, *there'll never be another night like this one,* he thought to himself. If only he could lay there in that moment forever.

They played until three in the morning, when they finally all conceded that they were tired and it was time to call it a night. They each took turns saying their good byes to Lucas before going inside.

Tommy shook his hand and told him, "thanks for the history lesson little man."

Dave approached him next and reminded him about girls, "Remember. Never send anyone else to talk to a girl for ya...be a man." He smiled at him and shook his hand before going inside.

Joe and Paul Cooper laughed with him a while as they reminisced about Mary Ellen and the telephone pole in the parking lot. Then finally Joe said to him, " And remember, Pop Rocks and Soda will make your stomach explode," gesturing at Jason the whole time for being a moron. Then both boys said good bye and rode their bikes home.

Finally Robbie found what he wanted to say to him, and gave it his best shot. He said, "You know kid. You're alright. You've been a good friend to Brett, and we always liked having you around here." He patted him on the shoulder and added, "Keep in touch." Lucas smiled as he walked away, then yelled behind him, "Call me next time you go fishin' for deer!"

Lucas, Jason and Brett found themselves sitting on the porch steps in silence.

"Okay, this sucks," Jason finally said.

"Sure does," Lucas replied.

"So listen," Brett started in, "You shouldn't come by here in the morning."

Lucas kept his eyes fixated on the ground in front of him.

"That'll be weird, ya know? We should just say...goodnight...right now. Act like it's no big deal."

Lucas nodded silently as Jason agreed. They remained in that same spot in silence.

Finally Lucas got to his feet. "It's late. Jason, let's head home."

Jason looked up at the boy with a great deal of surprise, then decided to just play along. He too stood up from the porch steps and gave a short, nondescript wave to Brett and began to walk away. Lucas smiled through pursed lips the way he always does when he's not sure what to do next, and followed Jason's lead. Short wave, and walk away.

A few steps from the porch, and something occurred to him that he had been dying to ask Brett since that first day they met. He ran back to his friend...his best friend.

"Something I just wanna know," he started.

Brett looked up at him with raised questioning brow.

"That first day we met. How come you never brought that up again? You never told anyone, or teased me about it. Why?"

Brett's brow changed as he looked at his friend with uncertainty. "Why would I? Why would I tease my friend about something that would embarrass him like that? And how it happened," he shrugged, "Well that's just none of my business."

Lucas stared back at him. The answer was just that simple...and maybe Lucas knew that all along, but it was the event that brought them together yet they had never spoke of it. Lucas felt his heart grow heavy in his chest. "You're the best friend I've ever had," he confessed. "I know you have lots of friends, and your bothers, but,"

Brett interrupted him. "Luke. Me too." Brett stood up and extended his right hand. "Call me when you get there."

Lucas shook his hand and sadly turned to walk away. Suddenly standing in front of him…one last time…the mangy brown dog. He sat in the parking lot between Jason and himself. Lucas froze one more time in the presence of the beast. *Why?* He thought. *Why is he here now? I was almost out of here with my dignity.*

The mutt walked over to Lucas and looked him straight in the face. Lucas stood perfectly still. Then the dog took one more step forward and placed his cold wet nose under the small boys hand. Lucas shied away from him, but then carefully placed his hand upon the brown dog's head and gave him a simple pat.

"Come on Snoot," Brett called out to him.

Lucas spun on his heels as the dog trotted away. "That's your dog?" he called out.

Brett grinned and nodded as the dog brushed past him in the doorway. He waved and went inside. Lucas laughed out loud and then continued on his journey across the grass with Jason Sharper.

At Jason's door they simply shook hands like men, said *See ya,* and he went inside.

Lucas walked slowly through the Manor. He took in every house, car, telephone pole, mailbox…every inch of Landit Manor. Then he walked right through his front door.

His parents sat up in their sleeping bags, as his mother called out to him. Lucas appeared in their bedroom doorway where they lay on the floor. "I snuck out my window, and played midnight football with the guys. I'm going to bed now," and he walked away. His parents looked at each other and decided not to fight. The morning would be here soon enough and he would be leaving every thing that he loved behind. That was punishment enough.

The next morning the Reed family took one more look through the house, packed the station wagon, and then climbed inside. They drove silently through the Manor. Turned Left on to English Road, and stopped at the sign. Lucas looked for Snoot and the other dog, but they were nowhere to be found. As the car turned left again heading out of town, Lucas' mother saw something out of the corner of her eye. Kids. Kids on bicycles!

"Look Lucas!" she yelled pointing out the window.

Lucas flipped around in his seat looking out the back window of the Station Wagon. There they were! Brett, Jason, Paul and Joe were riding their bicycles after them yelling and waving as the Reeds drove out of Hampton Mills, NY one last time….Snoot hot on their heels.

The End

www.ingramcontent.com/pod-product-compliance
Lightning Source LLC
Chambersburg PA
CBHW051824170626
46807CB00003B/1017

* 9 7 8 0 5 7 8 0 5 6 3 5 7 *